The
Shaver Mystery Magazine
Vol 1 No 2 1947

Richard S. Shaver
Alfred Steber (Editor)

SAUCERIAN PUBLISHER
Original Sources in Ufology

ISBN: 978-1-955087-49-0

9 781955 087490

2023, Saucerian Publisher

PROLOGUE

Returning to the classics in any genre is generally a good idea. This also goes for UFO literature. Rereading a book or reviewing old documents after ten or twenty years is a rewarding experience. You will discover new data and ideas you didn't notice before. The reason, of course, is that you are, in many ways, not the same person reading the book the second or third time. Hopefully, you have advanced in knowledge, experience, and intellectual and spiritual discernment. A good starting point is to reread the UFO classics to understand the more profound mystery of what happened during that era.

This title is scarce and hard to find these days. The Shaver Mystery Magazine originally was published by the Shaver Mystery Club. This newsletter published the first printed stories on UFOs and was a major forum for debates about the occult, Forteans, and Lemurians. As Ray Palmer promoted it: "dedicated to the further study of the hidden truths as presented in the fact-fiction stories by Richard S. Shaver..."

In essence, the Shaver Mystery is a collection of stories in which Shaver claimed to have discovered proof of an evil humanity in underground caverns. Shaver portrayed an alien race that resided in Earth's caverns before escaping, leaving behind two distinct populations of offspring: the "Teros," a benevolent group of humanoids, and the "Deros," or "detrimental robots," a vile race who tormented and devoured humans. The Deros were especially brutal to women. The tales encouraged the establishment of Shaver Mystery Clubs.

The present edition is an authentic reproduction of the original Shaver Mystery Magazine printed text in shades of gray. **IMPORTANT,even though we have attempted to maintain the integrity of the original work, the present facsimile reproduction may have missing letters and blurred pages, poor pictures due to the age of the original scanned copy.** This magazine has been formatted from its original version for publication. Great, but unpretentious, this issue is an extraordinarily rare symbol of what was going on in those early years of the modern UFO phenomena.

Editor
Saucerian Publisher, 2023

The SHAVER MYSTERY MAGAZINE

Being dedicated to the further study of the hidden truths as presented in the fact-fiction stories by Richard S. Shaver, made famous in the past three years in AMAZING STORIES magazine.

Subscription Price 50c per Issue

OBTAINED ONLY
THROUGH MEMBERSHIP
THE SHAVER MYSTERY CLUB

CONTENTS

Vol. I.   1947   No.2

EDITORIAL . . . . Page 4

READER'S SECTION
    By The Readers . . . . Page 5

MANDARK (Installment Two)
    By Richard Shaver . . . . Page 6

Frontispiece by H. W. McCauley

THE SHAVER MYSTERY MAGAZINE

is Published by

THE SHAVER MYSTERY CLUB
2414 Lawrence Ave.
Chicago, Ill.

Richard S. Shaver, *Editor*   Chester S. Geier, *President*

-:- NOTICE -:-

With this issue of the Shaver Mystery Magazine all one dollar subscriptions expire. Continuance as a member of the club, for research into the hidden and mysterious aspects of the Shaver Mystery, means only that further subscriptions to the club magazine is necessary. Putting this publication out is no easy task, and we will need the whole-hearted support of all members. If you sent a dollar in before, please re-subscribe now so that we may determine better the future cost of publishing the magazine. You will want to follow Mandark to its astounding end, so send us your subscription for the next two issues now . . .

         . . . Chester S. Geier

❧ EDITORIAL ❧

Among those who criticize me for what has become the "Shaver Mystery" are people who call themselves "religious", or who say they believe in the Bible, or who belong to this or that church, or who find me unscientific". Some have even gone so far as to say I blaspheme, that I am a Satanist, that I am an agent of evil. They say these things because of certain sex angles I use in my stories, in my articles, in my letters; because of such things as "blood-sucking" ancient "priests" and others who maintain their youth through this monstrous practice of drinking the blood of babies; because of certain "filth" I use in plain, outspoken words, the words that the dweller in the depths (of society as well as the caves) can understand; because of statements contrary to "accepted" science.

All right, let's take the Bible. What does it say? I won't quote, I'll just tell you what's in it—you can read it for yourself, to check. (If it is true that many "religious" people have never read their Bible—the basis of their faith!) The Bible tells us of giants; it tells us of regions deep within the earth, caves where living souls are tortured, or where they remain in a sort of "limbo" awaiting rescue; it tells us of space ships, or rocket ships (those that destroyed Babylon!); it tells us of dragons and monstrous humans lower than beasts—it tells us of the SHAVER MYSTERY, in different words, but with the same *meaning*. Read Shaver, then read the Bible. See just how many times the Bible agrees. Can you say that the Bible is without filth (King David, for instance) and without sex? For example how about Chapter 7, verses 1-10 in the Book of Solomon? The same sort of sex passages I've used. The Bible is a great book. It is the garbled remnant of a once greater book, the T book. The book of Life, of Integration, of Health, of Happiness, and of Life Everlasting. It was a book of T Science. It was no myth. It was TRUTH. It still is truth. Read it and see.

Am I a Satanist? Do I preach evil? Does the vicious ever see condonement in my stories? No. But I DARE to tell of a real Satan; I dare to expose evil that more pious people refuse to see because its existence (to be admitted) would shame them for not doing anything about it. I dare to show that there ARE vicious people and vicious practices, and eternal slavery of the foulest kind, from physical labor to vastly abnormal sexualities (and not all of them underground!) I try to cry out against them, to overcome them, to paint them as destroyed (in the future). Don't you think that SHOULD be done? Do you think it *will* be done, if no one ever mentions that they exist? And how can such mention be made if the correct words to understand are not used? People are complacent. They avert their eyes. They hold their hands over their ears. You've got to shock them. You've got to make them look, horrified at what they see. You've got to shout at them. That's your fault, not mine. Who is the blasphemer—the one who raises his voice, or the one who averts his eyes? Are you a coward that you cannot face the truth—or if I do not tell the truth, are you going to let me get away with it because you fear to be contaminated? You WILL be contaminated by evil, if you do not face it. Evil rides your back—it does not stand up to your face. If there is a mystery, avoiding it will not solve it. The mystery is why there is evil, filth, satanism, and all the other things I say that shock you. If we don't recognize the evil, we cannot solve the why of it!

In your secret mind, can you say that all your thoughts of sex are of a heavenly purity? Can you be honest to *yourself?* Or will you feign piety, declaim against me, who admits his thoughts are sometimes not of the purest? But WHY are they sometimes so? Because down in the caves there are evil dero with powerful stim machines and rays originally intended for PURITY of usage instead of debauchery of usage who debauch me and YOU with their rays, unknown to you. You think these things, and are ashamed! You are even horrified. You blame yourself. You rush to church to be purified. Of what? Of yourself? NO! Of something evil that influences **you**; of an OUTSIDE influence. I have told you what it is. I have not been able to PROVE it except with words. But does not the ACTUAL occurrence, effecting you, prove it? Are you willing to say that it is you, who do not want to be evil, who *are* evil? If YOU are that evil, then what is to be purged? YOU! ALL OF YOU! And that is annihilation. I say you can live forever, in glorious freedom and purity, but you do not, because your rights are stolen from you by that something that is NOT you, but which you cannot admit exists!

Therefore, no matter what ramification this Mystery takes, no matter how you may be "offended", no matter how much your even tenure of environmental thinking is disturbed, you cannot be justified in blind criticism based on dogma. You were "raised that way" and it prohibits thinking. THAT is one of the mysteries. HOW does it happen you were "raised that way"? Were you raised to evil? Are the dero raised to evil? MUST you be evil?

Then get off your trojan horse of illusion and face what can only be purported to be the "facts" (because no man has ever been able to tell where illusion begins and reality leaves off—or even what reality is) with an open mind. Don't let your mind tell your eyes what to see. Let your eyes, or senses, tell your mind what happens to them, and then let your mind weigh them and consider them. What it rejects honestly is "untrue"; what it accepts as logical, beyond any reasonable doubt, is "true".

What ELSE can you call KNOWLEDGE? What is TRUE beyond that which you "believe" to be true? Truth is HONESTY. I am trying to be honest. In my own mind, I AM honest. If your mind tells you I am not, then the mystery is solved for you, and you would be better off forgetting the whole thing now. If you have closed your mind, then close this magazine. It is devoted to a search, not a hiding beneath a bushel-basket of gilded virtue.

I have seen the caves. I know they exist. I am trying to prove it. And if you are a member of this club, you are trying to prove it. Opinions are not proof. If in your opinion I am all the things, or any of them, that I mentioned in the first paragraph of this editorial, very good, but it is not proof. None can see who have closed their eyes—and those who close them because they are offended will not see what is before them.

Richard S. Shaver

READER'S SECTION

Each issue we will publish as many pertinent letters to the Shaver Mystery as space allows. We urge all readers to contribute any facts, personal or otherwise, to help our research.

Dear Mr. Shaver:

The enclosed one dollar bill, will I hope, enroll me in the Shaver Mystery Club. If there are any other charges for magazines etc. please advise me and I shall forward the remainder.

In my first letter to you I mentioned an anecdote which pertained to one of Charles Fort's tales, and in reply you suggested I present my little story as possible material for the club mag. So here goes:

My father-in-law was one of California's most prolific composers and in respect to his memory and to members of his family as well as those of characters in this story, he shall remain anonymous. The story, never-the-less, is essentially true and I hope to be able to verify the story in the near future.

A few years ago father-in-law was regaling the members of the family with experiences of his youth in southern California while making his living as a pianist in a small orchestra which played for private dances, fancy balls, etc.

One evening while playing at the mansion of one of the local citrus barons, the members of the band, who were in reality, members in good social standing and as such were treated more as guests than as hired musicians, became rather high on champagne as the morning hours approached.

(Continued on page 25)

MANDARK

By RICHARD S. SHAVER

Continuing the Tremendous 200,000 word Novel
-- the true story of the Life of Christ

CHAPTER III

THE earth, Our Mother Mu, was spinning closer and closer in her inward spiral toward the sun which had captured her. On the surface the great ice sheets were melting, seas were forming, and floods swept across the rocky barren surface, yellow with the clay which had been buried under ice and under vast drifts of liquid air for untold eons.

* * *

I, Jehovah, Lord Ruler of Sabaoth, Elder planet afar, turned again to the big penetray vision screen which showed the surface far above. The last belated migration ships were blasting bright trails of smoke across the sky, leaving billowing brown rings as their pilots shifted the drives to greater and greater acceleration.

But I, by some freak of fate, must stay here on this cursed baby planet for untold years, under this deadly sun and see just what a sun does to life, for it had been so long since my race lived under a sun that the old work of that kind must be re-done. I had come to Mu for this express purpose.

This cruelty must be done, for it will result in vast good to the billions upon billions of our races in space, and Adam and Eve are but two, and their offspring will be twisted out of human character by the evil magnetic distortion of the sun's evil DE!

I looked at the intricacies of the great mechanism of the telesolididograph viso-ray, built by a race whose skill was borne not overnight, but over milleniums of effort by billions of technicians. The powerful magnetic field magnification, product of the science called "MAGIC" by the technicons of my race, would reveal any little life, any minute plant. It would even enlarge the view of a minute insect till the bug was spread over the whole twenty foot cubical screen in full, detail. And it accomplished that through the miles of rock overhead between me and the valley called "EDEN"! It would tell me just what the sun did, detail by detail, to man-life, as well as to all the other forms of life we would bring out of the abandoned hydro-ponic gardens of the caverns and plant in the great valley under the sun.

Swiftly I ran the great ray over the valley called "EDEN" above, studying the soil as the water drained away. As I studied I mused aloud: "Eden, once a frozen plain surrounded by mountains of ice, a place used for the landing of space liners too huge for the cavern ways—will soon be beautiful with the treacherous and deadly beauty of the life forms which will fill gradually with the radio-active poisons from the sun. Soon it is to become the home of the father and mother of all sin upon this poor cursed planet. Well, it is true it is an evil thing to do to two innocent children, but I know no other way to find out all the truth of evil degeneration under aging suns. But I do not like this job, I do not like it at all."

And in the garden, still a rocky expanse of bare wet soil, the plants of the great food gardens of the abandoned cities were set out in rows, each row of a kind, and within a short time the whole of the barren expanse was a carpet of wildly luxuriant and growing verdure. And a year swept by and fern trees were shooting tall, green spearheads at the sky that was now blue where it had always been black as night. And the two children, Adam and Eve, were released from the incubators where I had grown them from the seed left us by the departing Atlans. And they were the seed of the best woman of that city, and of myself, for it was my own son I condemned to this experiment—and the woman had consented, and gone her way. And Adam and Eve were turned out of the cave of the Treasures into the Garden of Eden, but the way into the cavern was left open, for the nights were still cold from the winds that had not yet died down from the first stormy broth of air, from the liquid air and air-ice which had covered the planet Mu.

● Illustration by Richard S. Shaver depicting life in the caves as he knew it.

AND I watched the two children playing in the Garden, which was a seeming paradise of lovely plants that all bore fruit, and of bright and harmless insects, and of beasts of every kind which were the pets of the departed people, and were all tame and harmless. And I could not help but feel sad, for I knew the terrible jungle of lust and sudden death and struggle for food which must in time be the end product of all my work. But it must "come to pass"!

And I guided the children and taught them to eat the fruit of the plants, and to pick the figs from the trees, and watched over them in every way that would not influence their character, which must be borne entirely from the natural influences of the combined magnetic fields of the earth and the sun above, which must of necessity be a natural self-borne character in every way—to prove our theories as to character correct.

For all we knew that Evil nature in man was due to disintegrant energy from sun, which the electric thinking machine, the human brain, in some cases inducts more strongly than in others due to an atunement in the magnetic fields of the cells, which in some resists these detrimental influences and in others fails to so resist and becomes instead an instrument for destruction in life— a life of fire, a life that accomplishes only what a fire would accomplish. But what we did not have was the details of this subjection to destructive flows of energy, and this mass of detail was what we expected to get from subjecting Adam and Eve to the new conditions of life under the sun that had captured the planet Mu.

But our job was vastly important. We faced the risks and we took our precautions against this infiltration of the inductive radio-activity from the sun, and we would win or lose our immortal lives.

Outside came a vast roar. Many ships filled the sky and dwindled into the small of distance. I knew it was the migration of the Atlans and the Titans from Mother Mu. But inside it was quiet, for we were in a cavern miles deep in the earth, and under-lying the valley called "Eden." For ages this valley had been a frozen nothing —now the sun had come into the life of Mu, and Eden had been chosen as the Garden where experiments in observation of sun-rays' effects upon life would take place. A very big, horned being, not entirely human in shape, was talking to me:

"Master, it seems a cruel fate for any life to be subjected to this evil sunlight till death. Is it wholly necessary?"

"Azrael, it is vitally necessary. We must have complete data on the effects of radio-active sun particles absorbed by the body under these aging suns. For this reason, all the data of our supposedly infallible scientific records is ages old. The subject has been neglected in the ages since we learned to live immortally in the shells of the planets of the dark spaces. The data which remains to us from the study of the cause of age is medically unreliable. We do not know if the men who made the records and observations of the experiments were honest and sincere scientists or not. Besides, this sun is made up of many elements not found in the suns under which the former work was done. The truth is, our immortal race is damned ignorant of its worst enemy —age. That is a situation that cannot go uncorrected for want of a little effort—or even cruelty."

The great horned being, who seemed to be my assistant in some mighty difficult job we had to do, went on talking:

"I understand, O my Lord. But they are sweet children, are Adam and Eve. It is hard to believe, to realize that so soon Adam and Eve must become hideous from old age. And that we must let them, must let the terrible poison from the sun devour their young lives. We know well what measures to take against the evil."

I shook my head. "The health of millions of far superior beings depends on the ruthless care with which we do our work, Azrael. A God can be too sentimental. For instance, many of the children of Adam and Eve will become Evil, cruel and untrustworthy. We know it, and must let it happen while we take notes, endless spools of record-wire of their thoughts, for all our police and medical men must know all the little signs of evil degeneracy in the young."

*   *   *

INTERIM

AND time passed on the face of the earth, and the sun turned and burned, and the earth, turned and swung in its orbit about the sun. And the sons of Adam and Eve multiplied as told in the bible. And I dreamed on within the mighty dream-mech of the Gods, with my faithful little Nydia tending, and she put records in of the time that passed, or put her own thought into the receptor screen of the mechanism, and the tales her people had told her of this time.

And the Latter-Gods rose and spread through all the caverns, and were mighty, but not wise as were the Elder Gods of the days of cold upon Earth's face. And because of their ignorance and their vice and their practices, they decayed and became as Devils within the earth, and the legend of Hell and its devils was borne of their custom of capturing and torturing men in their homes deep in the earth. And this was a terrible and an ignorant time upon earth.

* * *

CHAPTER IV

I AWOKE, and Nydia fed me, and said: "You must learn all quickly, for I do not know how long we may be able to stay here. The devil-rays may drive us away or kill us. So back into the dream-mech you go."

Time passed, a great deal of time. Twenty thousand years, in all. Their time measurement was very different from our own, and there is no way to tell you how long it was from the records.

There ARE records, as you may have gathered from other writings about this forbidden and hidden base of our past. Vast and complete records, in the hidden cavern cities that still exist. But they are not easy to read, being records of thought for the most part—a thought full of alien and multiform symbolism too great conceptually for our poor brains to grasp.

In this chamber which the two last High Gods of all earth had prepared, where for so long had been only silence, the tick-tock of a timing mechanism had begun. The pre-timer had functioned. . . .

For an age the pre-timer had weakened, for it was a device whose operation was based on the slow deterioration of a soft metal, as a fuse is based on the weakness of the fuse wire. Now at last it had parted and the final timer had begun its work. At the same time the soft glow of an emerald light filled the polished rock walls of the chamber. Otherwise there was still the silence of the sealed rock room, except for an occasional bubbling from the metal tubes leading to an egg-shaped container of a man's size at the side of the room.

On a low couch, at the wall, under the emerald light, lay the nude bronzed figure of a giant woman.

Time passed, the electric clock ticked, the bubbling sound went on at intervals in the hidden place. The giant woman's skin was soft and her arms spread as though to receive an infant.

A God's skin was never exposed to the rays of the sun, but only to the rays of their own making. Her head was very large, her hair soft and lustrous as living hair is soft and lustrous. She did not move. A year passed and no thing moved in the soft green light of that mysterious cradle of mighty life. There was only the tick, tock; the green light, the white hangings and the golden bronze beauty of the woman against the white.

Then the timing mechanism went off with a loud crack like a circuit-breaker. The door on the egg-shaped container swung open. Cradled within was a baby, a very big and very much alive baby, the nutrient fluids in which he had been immersed draining off him. He let out the usual cry of a newborn child and began to breathe the air of the chamber. He was the son of a strong and ancient race. He was their seed, left in the time capsule as a gift to all the people of Mother Earth, in return for their subjection to the terrible and certain death of the sun that had been ordained to the children of Adam and Eve by the necessity for study of the effects of the sun upon animals, including the human animal.

There are several races of Gods, many mixed races, and not all are of human form. This son of the ancient rulers of space was now the only hope of earth for a fair future. Born with the instincts and abilities of an animal far superior to ordinary man, he was able to care for himself even better than the normal wild animal is today.

Strangely, though the skin of his ancestors had been a bronze-white, the skin of the baby God was black as pitch. For the wisdom of the Elders who had put his seed within the incubator, had added a certain material to the nutrient which caused black pigmentation. Their purpose was to give him a better chance to resist the detrimental rays of the sun. It is startling to realize that nature has done the same thing for the black man of Africa that was consciously done for the Messiah.

This baby was the only Living God, on Earth!

He crawled about the chamber and soon found the still form of the mimic mother on the low couch. From her artificial breasts he drew nourishment, replenished from the hidden containers behind the mechanical figure.

TIME passed. Except for the low tick of the timer and the bubble of the nutrients in the hidden wall tanks there was no sound. The baby crawled endlessly about the great lonesome, prisoning and sealed room, finding solace only in the big soft breasts of the artificial mother. Another year passed; then the timer made another loud sound. Words came from a wall aperture. They were simple words, repeated over and over. On the wall-screen moving and delightful pictures illustrated the word's meaning.

The baby clapped his hands and watched the pictures, and as the pictures unrolled daily, he learned to talk, and as time went on and the automatic machani-disk changed the records to more advanced themes, his education really began. He learned why he was alone, and that he was the only living son of a mighty race on earth. That they had been forced to leave earth to flee the burning, aging sun, but could not bear not to give the people of old mother Mu some chance for a future. He was that "something", their gift to the future. He was the true Messiah. These books and records, these maps of their city caverns, their machinery, was all left him to serve his purpose.

To build again from the degenerate seed of Adam and Eve, destroyed in character and in health by the long centuries under the sun, their God-inherited intelligence reduced by the fearful sun DE through the years to the level of a stupid animal— reduced by the evil magnetic from their original greatness.

To build again an immortal race such as had peopled the earth before the sun had appeared, before they had succumbed to the evil degeneration force of the mighty burning atomic disintegrance overhead. Before they had succumbed to the evil, before their planet home had been captured by the great weight of the sun, life had been love and happiness. Now, after all this time, if it was possible to build such a life again even under the sun, that was his life job. He must succeed, the records repeated.

The Great Experiment of the God called "Jehovah" had been allowed to run its course, as they needed the observation of the full effects of a sun, from clean uninfected origin to final stages, upon a race of men. But their compassion had placed him here as an agent of their pity, to bring healing methods and the science of growth toward greatness again to man.

Most of the Gods left Earth at the same time, though a few did remain here and there on earth, for they were such ill-natured individuals from the already noticeable infection of DE, that none of the captains of the great migration ships would take them aboard. Too, they probably came long after, the junk dealers and scum of that tremendous civilization, to loot the deserted caverns of what valuables they might find.

These left-over, De-viles—or devil-gods, as man later called them, for their bodies were vile with the DE charge from the sun. (DE is from the ancient original language —is a shortened symbol for "disintegrant energy".) These devil Gods were the reason for the flight of the Gods, aside from the age the sun brought with it, for even a God could become a Devil if the Sun infection took his natural good-will and left the destruction compulsion of the disintegrant magnetic forces of the sun.

And the years passed in that green-lit chamber deep in the rock of Mother Earth, and daily the young God studied what had been written by the man-God who had left his seed as an offering to the great soul of Mother Earth and to her people. And if the God had not known that Mother Earth was a life herself, had a kind of existence as a being in her own right, it would not have been true that the young son of the Gods had been alive. For the ages of the Gods thought of all things as living things, though living in different ways, and they loved Mother Earth for they had ways of knowing her that have since been lost.

At last the young God was grown to a great size, and the voice from the wall spoke saying: "Go forth, and conquer the people who swarm over earth and make these people well again."

AND the young God went up out of the chamber FOR THE DOOR WAS NOW OPEN where had been no door before.

In the great cavern city of the OLD RACE his feet carried him among the endless empty mansions marveling at the work of his fathers. At the beauty that had been theirs. But he had expected all this for the cities were pictured in his books and in his mental records. But he had not expected this brooding emptiness, this time's death-of-time that hovered over all that wondrous handiwork. His heart sank for there was no life anywhere. And he turned on a great dynamo of the kind that run by a gravity focus and need no fuel. He directed the current through the See-ray mech, and looked everywhere about for people, but there were none that he could call men. Some small monkey-like things ran furtively from his bright vision, ray-beam and concealed themselves within a ray-opaque room, but he could not think that these evil-smelling things were men. At last he directed the great penetrative ray up through the miles of rock above him into the sunlight of that valley that had once been Eden. Now a great city lay in that valley, and the name of that city was Jerusalem, and the valley had risen to a plateau.

The voices and thoughts of the men of the city brought the knowledge of what men had become to him and he was sad, for men are not Gods, and the young God was surpassing lonesomeness for his his own kind. But there was good in them, and he could try.

There is no way to put two quarts of fluid in a thimble, and the young God found it impossible to tell the men of the surface anything. These people fell down and worshipped when he showed his image over the "projector-solidograph-communicator (telepic-mech)." But they could not understand even his thoughts when he caused the image beam to augment his thoughts near the men of the surface: They heard the great and mighty thought, yes, and knew only that a God stood before them, and they worshipped but he found no way to use them for an intelligent thing.

Too, they had great fear of his seemingly solid projection, for their traditions and their own experience had taught them to fear all such things as the work of Devils or of Evil Gods and they wanted nothing but to get far away from it. And young Yahveh could not understand this, for he did not know yet what had been happening during the thousands of years while he had slept. He had been taught everything up to the point of the preparation of the birth chamber, but then the chamber had been closed against all entry, and no one had corrected the records or brought them up-to-date for the Messiah. He did not know what had gone on, nor of the eons of time since his home had been built for the long embryo sleep. With a great sadness in him, the young God decided that he would have to raise his first followers from little children with the ancient penetrative beneficial rays to make them wise and strong and able to understand him. So it was that not only the Virgin Mary, but other women as well were told that they bore within them the seed of greatness. For the beneficial rays, penetrating the rock, beamed upon the unborn children within them and made them grow in a way that men had not grown since the Exodus of the Gods.

Mother Mary saw the radiant image of the beautiful young God near her in the night, and knew not what had been done, but only that a God had shown his love for her. The young God had turned to Joseph and said:

"Joseph thou son of David, fear not to take Mary thy wife unto thee, for that which is conceived in her is of the Holy Ghost. She shall bring forth a mighty son, and thou shalt call him "JESUS."

Now, when Jesus was born in Bethlehem, the young God of the deep caverns set over Bethlehem a great light like a star, so that man should know that the word of the Ancient Gods was fulfilled and that the son of God was born again. For he knew that men couldn't understand him, but that they would understand Jesus whom he planned to raise among them as the answer to the great promise left them of old, that he was sure.

AS the young Messiah, the only living God on earth, swept his great old see-ray around about in the night, as he watched over Jesus and set the star flaming above the stable cave where Jesus lay, he saw in the adjacent caverns a thing he had not expected to see. His teachings had not mentioned them as he saw them now. It was true he had been warned that some evil forms of life were to be expected—but the teachings had not prepared him for the sight of devils. And there were devils above him in the old cavern city, and they knew that he was there below them, and were preparing to kill him with one of the ancient weapons. Small and man-like things they were, but totally different from the men he had watched on the surface, for all their lives and many generations of their ancestors had been spent wholly in the caverns, which were for the most part dark now.

For the ancient cavern cities were not originally barren places of no light and no green leaves.

There was instead fresh air and beauty much as we think of as raised only in sunlight. They were, (instead of dark cavern holes), like great endless conservatories, abloom with an infinite variety of fecund gigantic plants, and above them burned tubes alight with designed actinic rays meant to promote growth without detrimental rays of any kind. A much more beautiful plant growth than is possible under the "natural", partly destructive rays of the sun. Much more beautiful than surface forests were the underworld forests of the God's planting. But after all the thousands of years that had gone by while his seed lay sleeping in the frozen sleepy waiting that his fathers had put upon him, the caverns were not healthy places to live anymore. The great beneficial rays which had made the caverns green with plant life, and had made the laughing people's feet light with immortal life, and their faces flushed with the health that is immortal,—had all gone out, or been put out by ignorance of those who now lived in the caverns. Portions of the caverns about him he refitted with new lights, and the ancient groves had bloomed again in all their immortal beauty under the hand of the young God, so that around him the ancient plant life had again become part of his life. So it was that the wisdom of the young God had made him able to fill the near caverns with the infinite beauty of the plant life of the original caverns. He had replaced the beneficial rays with new parts from the storehouses, the soil with preserved seeds, but most of the other, endless warrens of ancient borings were lifeless except for the furtive man-like things which the young God had not bothered to notice overmuch.

But these devils, which the Messiah now saw, were a sickish white from their life underground without the great old actinic ray lamps which had gone out, and sometimes their skin was mottled with brown lumps which were some strange fungus which grew in their skin here underground. Some of them were mis-shapen in various parts by the effect of using growth accelerating rays upon some parts without subjecting the rest of the body to the flows.

Some of them had spent the greater part of their lives within certain machines here underground, machines which were not understood by them but which were infinitely pleasant to stay within, and not coming out of such pleasure machines for anything but food, they were spindly of leg and arm, could hardly walk. But the horrors of their peculiar appearance was not the real horror about them. Reading their minds, the young Messiah was astounded, for in all the wisdom he had drunk in at the knees of his artificial mother—the thing he faced now across the screens of the ancient ray-weapons was not mentioned. For its thought was not thought! Pure detrimental energy plus reflection-thought (that is they perceived by reflection only, their surroundings added to their awareness only details, their thought was always that thought which they read in others) was only detrimental electric. The brain of a man is a battery, among other things, *that* the Messiah knew, but he had not known that it could be charged with full detrimental energy without death resulting. But here was proof of this, things like men whose brain batteries were charged to the full with detrimental electric. and all their thought was the result of this detrimental, and not the result of natural beneficial integrative flows from the brain cell electric at all. How could this thing be?

THESE were devils, his tardy memory came to life— waking from its astonishment at the first contact with fully detrimental thought. These are described as the end product of an age, many generations of degeneration, in a field of gradually increasing detrimental (electric de energy) content. As he watched their life, he deduced just how they came to be, and how they came to be able to live in spite of the detrimental electric which surcharged their bodies. (Electric eels "live", though the electric they give off in such quantities is detrimental to life). They lived within the antique beneficial rays, keeping them turned on all the time, but they did not know the difference between a useful ray instrument and a worn out one which gave off continuously increasing amounts of detrimental alloyed with the beneficial current. Hence they kept the pleasant-feeling beneficial rays going long after, centuries after, they would normally have been replaced with new metal. This mental result (of completely devilish thought) was due then to the long use of worn out beneficial and pleasure rays. Centuries of breeding and living in the detrimental field thus created had evolved a creature whose life was motivated wholly by the pervading destructive rays in which they lived.[10]

---

10 These "devils" no sooner saw the mighty figure of the black son of the Gods, than they began an attack upon him. It was an attack they soon wished they had withheld. They sent over his watching ray a charge of lightning which would have killed a lesser man, but he grounded the terrific charge before it reached him with a "shorter" ray (which is always fitted into ray instrument in the same way a fire extinguisher is hung upon a modern electric motor—or nearby. This "shorter" ray is a black conductive ray which acts as a fully con-

Young Yahveh waited no more to "study" these curious evil creatures, but wiped them out with flashing bolts of deadly energy. But he was not through with the "devils" of the caverns, for even as those died who were before him, others in the far reaches of vision took up the attack upon him, and the rock about him was a flashing, whirling pattern of lancing, darting arrows of penetrative ray from many directions.

He had precipitated an attack by hundreds, by a tribe of the dero. Throwing up a heavy fan of the black "shorter" ray before him, he swiftly retreated down to the depths that had bore him. He knew that this deep chamber was shielded by dense and impenetrable materials—that no ray could reach him there. Then, too, there were weapons more familiar to him, and periscopic sight by which he could watch and kill without being exposed.

The young God took several days, now, to study these cavern dwellers, for he was now understanding that they were the greatest obstacle before his plans for men. They had the antique weapons, and generations of them had passed down the methods of use which they had learned. Reading their thoughts, and taking record on the multi-recorder of every head in range of his ray, he soon had a complete cross-section of their life upon his spools. Taking the spools of wire from the recording mech, he realized that this deep crypt below the ancient city would always be his retreat in time of need—his only real home. There he spent his time studying the records of the thought of the devil people.

CHAPTER V

BENEATH Jerusalem the Golden lay the ancient city of the past Gods of earth, unknown to those above. It was entered by one great tube from the south ways, to all other ways the tubes had been closed by centuries of work to seal the underworld city from attack.

Over this entrance tube straddled the great Palace of Satantes Onderde, the ruler of the degenerate race who now peopled the ancient grandeur of underworld Jerusalem. Slim, swarthy, bearded, hook-nosed and elegant with the inheritance from a long line of absolute rulers over the terrible power of the God-weapons of this great empty city—a city peopled only by dwarfish men and women who were mostly his virtual slaves—rich with the accumulated stores of an age of terrible preying upon the surface world and upon the less formidable powers of the underworld—Satantes had one possession he valued above all others. This was his daughter, Lila. What little softness and human qualities still existed in this degenerating race was lavished on their children, and Lila's life was a pampered one.

Fancy that you are a woman. Your nude, white soul dances voluptuously before the background that is the flowering garden of your sense. Your hungry ego leaps within you at the ramparts of desire. Now you are "Tithea."

Tithea was the mother of the Titans, named after her. The Titans of the far past were the forbears of those worms of the present, called "man". Tithea is also the name

---

ductive flow, grounding any ray energy it touches).

There is a lot more to the understanding of the ancient mechanism's deterioration producing the devils, but it takes a while to explain. They lived in a constant bath of the ancient pleasure rays by habit, their great potency making life a constant ecstasy, and they had so lived for endless centuries. The gradually deteriorating mechanisms had induced greater and greater amounts of disintegrant electric-flows from the sun's terrible fields of magnetic.

As their bodies became accustomed to these flows, the phenomena of degeneration became accelerated in them. This functioned more greatly in the head than other parts of the body, because they spent many hours a day peering over the old penetrative rays at surface people and at each other. The disintegrance centered thus about the head, and the rest of the body made up for the energy losses by its production of natural integrative energy flows, hence the devils lived on. But the brain, so used to detrimental rays and energy flows that it could not generate sufficient thought energy to think with, at last succumbed and let the DE flows dominate the thought processes instead of its own product, the natural flows of thought energy. This synthetic detrimental thought-flow became habitual, then hereditary with the deros, they could not think without an old ray to peer into. The resulting flows of energy activated their defunct brain, while the conveyed thought from the person in the view screen gave them their reflected thought to which they reacted detrimentally without adding anything to the thought but the detrimental impulse. Thus only a reflected pseudo-thought was left them in place of normal created thought. No matter what the thought, it always finished within their heads in a detrimental conclusion, or a totally innocuous conclusion—kill, or nothing.

given earth, our mother, in the ancient tongue of the Titans.

To them, our mother earth *lived*, and her soul sent out her fecundity into each of them, (just Station XBQ sends out its music and commercials in modern times.)

Woman was her especial receiver, the instrument designed to display Tithea's message of life and beauty to man. That fecund sensing of the central will to procreate, that is the soul of woman; and that soul is but the reflection of an ancient being, our mother Tithea, **called** in later times "Mu", and now called "Earth", and forgotten as **being anything but a round chunk of rock upon which we crawl.**

To the Titans, each woman was Tithea. Some sensed her with a stronger perception, knew her command to procreate, to bring forth a future—these were the mothers of our race.

Such a woman is known for her love for all mankind. For her goodness, her mercy, her charity, her sweet womanliness.

Such a woman Lila was *not!* That soul that mother earth's being breathes into each of us was *not* present in Lila, was not heard. To all-apparent seeming Lila was a good counterfeit. But nothing in her inner-self ever heard the commands of the soft-voiced mother of all.

Today she strolled in the metal garden and dreamed of the past. She was a dream-maker and a slave to the practice of dreaming. When she dreamed, she did it with the help of a female slave or a young male slave trained to operate the antique records of the thoughts of the past, (which are called by those who do not know what they are—"dreams"). They were not dreams, but records of the ancient life, and they were so filled with intense impressions of the wonderful life of that time so far past that they seemed to these ignorant people like dreams, and were used for that purpose only—to escape from the misery and horror that was their own handiwork around them,—into a world where everything was, comparatively, perfect. They are so used, those tremendously valuable records of a life so far above our own, even today.

She was dreaming of a far-off planet, where the ancient cities were filled with life, and around her the metal trees breathed into a new synthetic life. The moon walked softly overhead, though this was the ever-dark of the underworld, and beside her walked a dream image of a mighty youth of the far past, infinitely stronger and more beautiful than any man now living. He talked in that forgotten tongue, in a voice that was rapture to her, and she would not stop the dream for all the wealth of Jerusalem the Golden, above.

AS she walked, lost thus in the lovely projections of a forgotten time and a world that exists no more, with the young grace of her youth upon her, and the augmentation of her bitter-sweet, evilly beautiful being making her an irresistible creature, the augmentation that is a part of the antique record-mech beam connection with her body making all that was woman about Lila many multiples of strength by electric augmentation, as she walked thus with her mind occupied with the vital beauties and thoughts of a people so far superior to her own tainted heritage,—she was, to all seeming, a superior being.

The young God from below swept his far reaching space-vision televisor-communicator-solidograph rays into the metal garden which he knew was the area around the strong-hold of the ruler of the men with whom he fought.

"The King-Devil's daughter", thought Yahveh savagely, seeing Lila.

But he was looking at what appeared to him a bit of the life of a rich and cultured kind similar to the ancient days. This was not true, but the projections of the dream machine about the form of the young and not unlovely Lila made her seem a real woman from the past of his father's time to the young Godling.

The heart of Yahveh was terribly and instantly stricken, for to see what appeared to be a real flower among all the thistles of life that were the "devil people" was somehow pitiful and appealing. To desired this Lila suddenly, for woman was to him unknown, and though he knew this Lila was the daughter of the leader of those who stood between him and fulfillment of the purpose of his life.

The solidograph projector at his touch sent his image into the metal garden, and Yahveh walked too beside Lila, eclipsing the ghost from the past who was making ghostly synthetic love to Lila, and Yahveh whispered into the shell-pink ear of the dark-tressed Lila, telling her of his lonely life and of his sudden need of her.

And for Lila, young, but not inexperienced in the ways of love; her mind filled with the dream images of the far past, this sudden projection of a living presence into her lonely garden of ghosts was fulfillment such as her inner desire had never hoped for.

Lila heard and understood who this was, for she had heard of the mighty wisdom-worker who had killed so many of her father's men—and her young bones thrilled to the inmost marrow to see for herself the beauty, the strength and majesty of which she had heard but whispers from her father's men.

He was so like the mighty people of the dream records who were seen today nowhere else. Her knowledge of the ways of the machines told her that this projection was not imaginarily doctored, as was the custom of the present day-makers of new dreams, but was real and true and honest.

She knew that this man was a living God from the far past, somehow magically appeared in the present, and she knew that he lived not too far off. So it was that Lila was one of the first to make the pilgrimage to the new God.

Lila made her slave swear to keep her secret, and to watch over her with a long-range ray while she took herself into the endless dark of the far caverns. These were fearful to her for many and very real dangers, but Lila drove herself on, her desire going before her, to the place where the wonder-work of the young God had made the green gardens again, and brought the brilliant synthetic sunlight from the restored power plants which had once raised food and grown gardens of beauty for a tremendous city.

THERE the odd and unknown fruiting trees grew again as they did in the dream records, the birds lived and sang in the branches of the trees, the very lovely flowering and fruiting trees of varieties of the old-time which the Prince of the Latter Dark had found the seeds still alive, in frozen life-storage as himself had been in his incubator.

The great blossoms filled the air with a perfume such as could only exist in Hevi Enn,[11] Lila mused.

Her young wilful feet carried her still in an unbelieving, irresistible dream, to the deep caverns below the gardens where the might of the young God had his stronghold.

Lila was not a woman, she was a strange and beautiful little monster with a terrible heredity of madness and evil. She could act like a human until opportunity presented for her to act her real nature—then the fires of Hell burst from her in deeds, in horrible acts.

Her nature was not fully understood by Yahveh, who for all his record acquired wisdom was still an innocent, virtuous youth, unaware of the reality of the Evil in this terrible world his time-swallowed parents had marooned him upon. May his Father forgive him his mistake.

The cunning Lila swayed her subtle young dancer's hips just as she had so often in the shameless dances of the palace, as her father's numerous concubines had taught her. Her gold-slippered feet carried her gracefully down and down toward the watching desirous eyes of the woman-hungry son of the Gods. Her firm young breasts were sheathed slightly in a halter of gold lace, and her bare, sinuous dancer's midriff, slender as a virgin's, tapered into a pair of hips such as only those whose ancestors have been devotees of stim-ray stimulated love for an age inherit. Low on those sensuously swaying hips a golden circlet of the cunning ancient jeweled work hung, holding from little dangling jeweled clasps, a skirt of diaphanous silken material, sparkling all over with seed pearls, and with rubies worked into patterns of flowers, the leaves a glowing green twining through the whole.

She was utterly seductive as she entered the chamber of mighty ray-cannon where

---

[11] Hevi Enn seems to have been a famous city planet of the Elder race—always referred to as the place most desirable to live—was a heavy planet, very fecund of growth—very healthful—very wonderful.

Enc. Britannica—Vol. 11, p. 178, Ed. 1907.

All over Europe fireside tradition tells of women who haunt lonely places, where they are seen to dance, to spin, to comb their long hair. They cause inexplicable diseases, epilepsy and St. Vitus dance, THEY HAVE A KINGDOM UNDERGROUND — WHITHER THEY ALLURE THEIR LOVERS, they appear with fatal gifts at children's births, they steal the children of mortals away, and leave changelings of their own. Our fathers dreaded them as the GOOD FOLK, the highlanders called them "the Folk of Peace"; in Greece they are "nereids;" in Servia—"wills;" in Bretagne—"Korrigans;" in Russia—"Rusalkas." The degenerate nature of these legendary people can be attributed to the fact that subterranean air is thirty times as radioactive!

the young Yahveh must keep an unsleeping vigilance now or pay with his life.

He turned to watch the small, wilful, unafraid feet of the daughter of the distant Ruler enter his home. His thoughts were a mad turmoil,—he knew this was not wisdom, to allow her to come here, but all the strength of him was ensorcled by the very augmentation with which he had watched her approach,—reading, instead of her thought, the dreams that had temporarily usurped her diamond hard, cruel "reason" that was not reason, but another terrible thing.

As she made to approach him, he held a small hand dis-globe upon her, the aperture pointing at her breast, saying—"Stay where you are, Lila Onderde, I have allowed you to enter, but I am not to be fooled. What is it you want here beside myself?"

LILA'S voice was honey-sweet, and her body did all those things the palace houris and her own imagination had taught her from so long watching of other lovers over the telaug's beams, and somewhat she knew from experience, who is the best teacher. Her arm raised in half supplication, all the soft roundness moving gracefully, she stood higher on her toe-tips to thrust her hips a bit forward, and little shivers of apprehension mingled with delight ran over body visibly. "Tis but to see you for myself, and make sure you are no dream-conjure, but a real God-man such as the ancient dreams do show us. Now that I see you are truly such, here I will abide till you drive me away. Know you not there are no such men as you on earth anymore? There is no woman by your side. I will be her, your woman, till another replaces me, and count my life well spent if it be but one day."

"Your people are to me as devils. How do I know you will not be a devil to me, and slay me in my sleep if I let you stay?"

"Put chains upon me when you sleep, lock me in a store-room, do what you will—but keep me here beside you. I would learn the true magic which only such people as you are ever knew—I would breath the same air you breathe, I would know you as I know myself—I care for nothing else!"

"They are good words, but how do I know they are true? How do I know you come not at your father's command, to slay me by some ruse?"

Lila inched closer, for she had a better argument than words, if he would but let her use it. Yahveh kept the deadly ray-globe opening pointed at her breast but that did not stop her advance. He could detect no thought of ill-intent toward him within her, but he knew that it might arise at any time. With another hand, he swept a great old multi-purpose ray-cone around from its outward pointing, and from it swept a great ray of delight upon her, held her in an ecstasy such as none of her own stim artists had ever evoked from the more worn-out and over-used machines of her fathers. No moth can resist the light any more than a human can resist the delight from the antique pleasure rays—and Lila walked now as the moth flies toward the light. If only young Yahveh had understood fully the nature of this woman! But he had been fooled by the glories the old dream mech record had placed about her form in this imitation moonlight in her metal garden. And his arms caught her up within the stimulation of infinite delight of the beam, and love welled up within them both as it cannot help but do within such beams, and for long hours the warning signs from his many electric eye-beams went unheeded. And when his senses returned to the danger about him, he swept the visi-rays through every cavern above and found Satantes Onderde, the Ruler, raging toward him with an army of vast, old, wheeled machines about him, and the dis-rays heating the outside of his impervious metal-walled retreat to incandescence (opaque to the the penetrative rays which otherwise travel through rock as through air). For it was a shame to the ruler that his daughter had gone to an enemy, and his rage knew no bounds.

As Yahveh leaped to his vast ray-cannon, and sent the dread bolts blazing into the ranks of her own father's men, Lila stepped to his side and with a smaller but as deadly a beam, cut the spinal cords of men she had grown up with, sending dozens into death before Yahveh had slain the greatest part and the Ruler, her father, fled precipitously from the sudden blazing death that had overwhelmed him.

Yahveh found it strangely ominous that this Lila was able to kill her own people for love of him. He did not realize that she would just as cheerfully kill him too, when something better offered which he stood in the way of obtaining.

So it was that the cunning wiles of her woman's clever body were worked by Lila upon Yahveh's woman-starved and powerful man-nature, he could not help but be entranced by her when he had never had woman near him before.

WHEN his thought was elsewhere, Lila reveled in plans for the things she would do to and with him when he was in fact her slave—in chains and in her father's house—or some place where she was the power and he the servant. When his mind was listening to hers she made beautiful love talk, cunningly laced with her own feminine enchantment, of little coo's of mental urges toward sexual thinking, and the young God was not loath to listen. But no one, not even a Yahveh, a God's son, could resist all the snares this distorted nature of the earth under the evil sun was laying for his mighty mind. Lila happened to be the most dangerous key to unlock the armor of Yahveh's God-given strength, but there were others.

Love did spread through all Lila's body and her mind was nearly won, but could such an intent live for long in her body? Lila was a girl who had killed many slaves for the fun of hearing them scream! She was also a girl who had been kind to those who were faithful to her, which was unusual in their terrible life. She was also a girl who had never been thwarted in her will by any but her father.

So they met, the young daughter of the ruler of the race of devils, and the young son of the Gods of old time. The ancient science was in a large part a knowledge of the causes and refinements of pleasure, and the ways of life's delight were like a backbone to the antique science, for even frivolous natures found in time that only by the study of science could they learn how to produce the infinite delights of synthetic pleasure impulses. So it was that the young God understood what would best please Lila and as their natures drew closer in friendship, the pride and evil will of her was softened still more by the mental work of young Yahveh within her mind. But these flashing, ever-changing forms of beauty that were the thought of Yahveh within her mind were not more entrancing than the simple yet awe-inspiring tones of his God-like voice.

"You have a strange beauty, Lila, your mind is not so dull as the others of your race. Think of yourself, so that I may know you by listening to your thought."

Lila habitually thought well of herself, it was a favorite occupation of her to whom the society of others was for the most part denied except during festivities or when she stole some male companionship by stealth when her father was elsewhere. She thought of her "self" putting on her arms the ancient golden ornaments of a beauty of workmanship so fearfully more than mortal—of dressing her form in the transparent olden gleaming fabrics that were found in the sealed closets of the cavern homes—of her hair pinned full with the gems that are like no others on earth's surface—the Hellstones, the firepearls and the great green emeralds from the vaults below the caves, she thought of her dancing which was a part of her life. And, too, she thought of the fierce pleasure of torturing her slaves, and of beating to death the low class people when they opposed her wishes in the slightest, even when they were obeying her father's orders. All these things she thought of and of her father's savage court, where the wealth of an age was displayed, which he had taken as toll from those who passed the gates to the underworld. She thought of the fierce games they held in the underworld circus where men fought with beasts after the Roman fashion, and where enemies captured or thieves taken were crucified for a spectacle. She thought of all these things and much of it was horrible but some of it was beautiful. The worship of Satan was particularly interesting to the young God and he made her review for him the ceremonies of their worship of the Dark One—where a woman's naked body was the altar and the sacred Icor from the God's stores was imbibed by all before the altar. The ceremonial red devil masks, the whole barbaric spectacle of the hidden devil worship of the caverns was watched by Yahveh with a dawning comprehension.

FOR the immense age of this evil fixation in the minds of all the cavern people under this line of rulers, and of other groups he discerned existed, from her thinking, and how the need for ceremonial blood shedding was born and bred in them. And he watched her pleasure as the life of the human sacrifices spouted from their breasts, and as the babe of the ceremony was killed and a bit given to eaten of by all. He realized that this was a survival of the ancient practice of eating children and the drinking of children's blood by those evil ones. He realized that they know enough of the old science to know that young blood would keep them younger. (A knowledge still a cursed practice by some, it is said.) All these things she displayed and he watched in her mind through the mighty telaugmenter which missed no slightest detail of her mental pictures. And she was innocent of the nature of the Godling and showed it all to him unknowing that the pictures might estrange his heart from her forever. For her life had been a hideous fabric of unconscious evil, of pleasure in evil things, and her mind was an heritage of evil intent, though her form was that of a beautiful young girl!

And Yahveh, realizing the danger to him that she could be, still knew that he might have need of such a hostage to the ruler of the men who fought him daily.

Now Yahveh tried to teach her, the young daughter of the devil race, the ways of wisdom. But her mind was like the other minds of the devil-race, so fixed in pattern from her heredity and upbringing that she could not understand. The way a rabbit jumps is inherited from an age of rabbits jumping and a rabbit can progress no other way;—so it is with evil minds, when they are wholly evil, they are the result of ages of doing evil. Their children and their children's children can think in no other way.

When alone, Lila thought long how she could take this young God's wisdom and have it for her own. And at last she had a plan, but she thought not of it when he was hearing her thought, and he knew it not.

Yahveh's failure lay in not realizing how fully murderous a little monster he had captured. Her mind was capable and contained the intricate instincts of seduction and entrapment. Her skill lay in mental subtleties of an immense inherited art from an age of devious thought of the rulers among dero people, people armed and ready to kill, and to be controlled only by the greatest artist of beguiling mental posturing among them. Such were her forefathers, imitators and thinkers and great men in their way, but their way was not human. Their way was an increasingly evil one as the whole people degenerated into the evil that was Hell, and the source of the Legend of Hell. The life of these deros was the same as the Hell of which the ancients and the medievals have written, and those whom Yahveh faced were the survivors of an age of hideous and merciless struggle among the mad but cunning men of the caverns, in those parts where the gradually increasing radioactivity of their mechanisms, used generation after generation, contributed the primary cause to their increasingly evil natures. The lush and perfect life-force mechanisms which the Elder race had left, to fill the caverns with all the means of a rich life without effort; had served but to support a seed-bed of future deviltry.

Yahveh learned that there were many such everywhere in the vast network of tunnels, roads and cities which was the Elder world (as it is still called today). Many kinds of groupings had taken place in the twenty thousand years since the Gods had left Earth. In the caverns many people had come to look and stayed to live. Some had degenerated into these devil people, others had become what the legends tell us of as the "Latter Gods". But there were not many of these better races of the underworld in this part of the underworld. There were left only these Devil-people in scattered groups through all the ancient cities.

AS he read the mental records from the Devil race he learned that for many centuries they had been playing "God" to surface men. Everywhere about Asia and Africa and Africa Minor and in other places, as well, which they knew of through their wide use of the communication apparatus. He learned that the holy temples above, raised by the people in veneration of the memory of the True Gods, were used by these devil races to provide their food and other things they delighted in. Young virgins they took up mystically by the use of the rays, the levitators used by the original Gods for lifting great weights or launching ships into the space-ways were used by the devils for thievery and worse. They spirited people away into the caverns for slavery or prostitution or something far worse. The ancient mech was used to produce mystifying miracles to keep the religious surface men generous in their giving to the temples, where they took up the food with a levitator or made it to vanish with a teleport mech ray silently before the eyes of the worshipping multitude. All this was angering to the young God who had been carefully reared by the designed thought record method of education to have a strong sense of right and justice in preparation for his career of conquering ruler of righteousness, and there was nothing right about the whole devil race fattening on the deluded men who paid their surface agents—the priests and the temple slaves. They had a real hell—and *had* had for many centuries—where the men of the surface who saw through the deviltry and tricks were taken, there to suffer for a lifetime of agony in the ancient healing machines. Putting a man into one of these and fitting it with a device which wounded him as fast as the medical rays healed him; they made a perpetual torture device out of a healing ray mech. A man suffered the agonies of death over and over for endless years. Their Hell was like that, provided ready made for their dero minds—a place where a man could be tortured for years without death being able to provide release. So they really *had* a Hell for those who did not pay them tribute, and their priests did *not* lie in telling the people of its horrors.

He learned that they considered the surface people as their "property," as one considers cattle one's property and that they called the surface men "meat people" and themselves they called, oddly enough, the "efrits" or "Affreets." It was a word sourcing in Arabia, which had come to mean "devil" to surface man.

Yahveh had dreamed, shut up in his cradle chamber, of the time when he would be released from his training and meet men. He expected them to be living in the cavern cities, and to be using the ancient machines to some advantage, and speaking the ancient tongue. But he found a people he could not even talk to, for the ancient tongue was no longer used. And when he spoke to the surface men telepathically, if they were not frightened away, they thought is was their own thought talking, or else that it was an "Affreet" deluding them with lies—which "devil" voices they were used to and either paid no attention or went to the priests to have the devils driven off. This was sometimes efficacious as what government they had, worked through contact with the priests and they sometimes obeyed the priests because their food and money came through them.

He found a people stupid, unlettered and duped by a degenerated cavern race who made of their life a burden and a misery to them. And in this race of cavern people around him he could find no good thing, nothing he could use as a rung in the ladder he was meant to build to the future for all men.

EXPLANATORY FOOTNOTE :—

The ancient chamber where he had lain asleep for so long was originally a kind of fortress. It was not an arsenal of ancient weapons placed there for his use by those who left him. It was well protected in all ways from either penetrative rays or worse weapons. Far below the cities in the caverns, it was impregnable. But between the young God and the surface lay the cavern cities and in those cities dwelt an evil race, the descendants probably, of the devil Gods who had been refused passage on the ships leaving Earth in the original migration of these races of immortals from the aging emanations and showers of radioactive atoms from the sun.

Between him and the surface were the thousands of killer men and women of Lila's tribe, who had weapons and a lifetime of experience in their destructive use, and, they would kill him the moment they saw him he knew from reading their minds over the telaug. Above this killer race of people was the surface of its city of Jerusalem and surrounding cities. These swarmed with a life of a more natural and kindly kind, and the nearest city of the surface above him was Jerusalem.

These races of the higher caves above him had a civilizaton of a kind, but it was wholly parasitic upon the surface above—the men of the caverns did not work, but preyed upon the credulous people above by all manner of tricks. Witchcraft, "son games" such as the ancient "demon lover" racket, magical and mystical illusions they worked upon the surface men, by means of the miracle mechanisms, provided them all with revenue. But they all paid tribute to the holders of the entrance. This was their misfortune that the smartest and quickest among them had seized upon all the rocky cavern entrances and sealed them in, and nothing could pass out or in without paying tribute of most of its value to the holders of the Gates. So that all their monopoly of the wizard work of the past was nothing but a slavery to the holders of the entrances. For them they worked all their wool of magic and God pretense upon the credulous people of the surface, and the profits from all their work went to these holders of the openings, the rulers. So that these who held the ancient magical gates, that opened only to certain sounds upon a pitch pipe, or are ray activatic, were the rulers of all the life of the underworld, and the keepers of the vast secret.

"THE VAST SECRET" .

It is long that they have kept that secret, and their sons and the sons of their sons have kept that secret, and lived from the revenues of the trade and tribute that passed through the gates to the underworld—to "Hell" to "hades" to "sheol." To the "Halls of Pluto," the "Realm of Satan," the underworld has had as many names and rulers as there are fish in the sea. For the underworld is everywhere about the globe, just as is our surface life. But to our learned historians all this is and has always been just "fairy tales." But the truth is vastly otherwise than a "fairy tale," and much more wonderful, and much, much more horrible. And the loss is greater to us all than any writer can put in words.

Under Jerusalem the caverns were called "Sheol" and the ruler happened to be named "Satantes". But the forms of the name "Satan" are many, and in the underworld Satan is as numerous as is JOHN up here, so that *which Satan* was, *which* is hard to fathom from the fragmentary records of those times one runs into down there.

The Messiah, Yahveh, the son of the Gods, had great power in his place in the depths, immense weapons and generators—but they were immovable and fixed in their base. It was an ancient arsenal of space weapons, and the range was vast, but he could not leave the place or the devil race above him would kill him.

THERE in the soft beneficial light of his father's creation, he and Lila studied the records of the thought of the devils, and of the thought of the men above surface, Yahveh thought upon what he could do to fulfill the purpose for which he had been created. But Lila pondered another matter, when she could, how to have this man her own, instead of the other way around. Lila pondered how to have his wisdom, which he would not teach her for fear her evil nature would rise above his control of that nature, and whelm him with a demon he had made as powerful as himself.

Thinking such thoughts, Yahveh searched the surface earth above with the long range rays, and among the Jews above he found a pregnant woman named "Mary." He projected his image by television ray-beam to her, a ray projection which is three dimensional to the sight.

The image which the ancient machine projects can also talk and seem in all ways like close vision of a real person—and the image of the God-like being told Mary that she had been selected to become the mother of the "Saviour." For the Messiah, prisoned as he was in his impregnable fortress by Satantes' men, knew that he could yet work his will if he prepared men to do as he bid them. He started such preparation with the babe in the womb, for he had absorbed his forebears disregard for the evanescence of life, and from studying the old records had absorbed the ways of thought of the immortals. In truth he knew that he would die of old age, in time, just as people of less directly immortal lineage died, but he had *not* formed the habit of thinking and planning that way. So Yahveh started his education of the agents he planned to use in his campaign with the babe in the womb, not consiously realizing that he would be an aging man himself before the child had come of age. Consciously he knew he did not want to use men he didn't "know" as well as he knew himself, and that requires time. And the full extent of this urgency to accomplish his work before age and death laid him low had not come into his mind as yet.

Yahveh did not propose to build power for stupid and greedy minds, for ordinary men to usurp and turn to evil ways. He commanded Mary to raise the Child by instructions which he would give her from time to time.[12]

As you know, Harod was King of the Jews at this time.

Satantes Onderde and his devil people of the subterranean wonder city, having tried in every way to rid themselves of Yahveh and his immense cunning and aptness at the game of ray-warfare—this huge black-bodied menace of a man that had out of nowhere from beneath them—had decided to thwart all his efforts at organization, and so cripple his future power. The young Godling was himself too much for them, what would he be when he had surrounded himself with able warriors?

So Satantes put a conductive beam upon the head of Herod, and kept it there. Over this ray went constantly Satantes commands, Satantes responses to all the things Herod heard or thought about. As Herod had little mind to speak of, and what there was of it was much like his (Satantes) own, this was not difficult. Herod's mind was as easily swayed by detrimental flows of energy, and productive of little thought of Herod's own design. Making Herod speak by such control, sending his own thoughts strongly over the ray to Herod's mind, (which in those days was called "possession" and was well known among men—though today we call it madness and shut the innocent victim up in a cell) they (Satantes) caused Herod to command the death of

---

12 The truth about Jesus' birth and life may have been otherwise, according to some evidence, but name and date are not too important. The history of the Church itself admits that the book, the "Bible", has been changed several times in its life, its long existence has made it liable to many mutilations. Just what the original book may have been is as interesting speculation.

FOOTNOTE—Ray fighting :—
These ray battles have gone on, in the caverns, since the earliest times, right down to the present day. I have seen half a dozen of the modern secret ray battles—always going on all unknown to the supposedly peaceful surface world (although their fate was being decided by desperate battles) and there is no more thrilling or terrible sight on earth than to see the terrible weapons of the Gods in action, and in action right under the feet of peaceful American cities full of people, unknowing.

These ray groups are as fixed a pattern of activity—filled with as great an antiquity of custom—as ever were the ancient sword and battle—and shield days of war. It is almost impossible to describe, for there is so little known to you with which to compare the antique weapons or methods of another race and culture as time than our own.

every child born in Bethlehem that year. Thus they hoped to stop the creation of any more such children as the great black man of the depths who was killing so many of them.

THERE were dozens of these children whom the busy young Godling had treated with beneficial energy flows, and if left to develop, Bethlehem and Jerusalem would have raised such a crop of superior young men as no city of earth has seen since written history began. But this stroke of the Devils in using Herod as their tool cost Yahveh all but one of the little proteges, and he was put to it to save even this one from the many soldiers.

The Messiah got his rays through their obstructing barriers of ray force to warn Mary and Joseph, and to tell them where to take refuge. He guided their fleeing feet, Mary and Joseph and the little Christ child—to a great opening down to a deserted cavern city in the desert, which none of the devil race had as yet inhabited. There Jesus and his father and mother lived for some years. In our history of the Bible of the surface world this period is called "the Egyptian flight of Joseph."

But in the endless warrens below the rocks of Mother Earth, the Messiah of the Cavern life was not unnoted, and his fame spread swiftly over the long range talking rays. Slowly, the wiser of the far caverns, even so far north as Ancient Brittany, moved to join this new leader.

The Messiah is now about ten feet in height. His great stature results from the giant size of his father and mother. His father was Jehovah, the scientist responsible for the great experiment of which we men of earth seem to have been the subjects.

His great black shoulders rippled with the muscles which the Titan system of exercises had given him. His eyes—of great size due to his life in the semi-dark and in the beneficial rays of his cradle chamber's equipment, flicker swiftly about the array of mighty mechanisms with which he keeps an eternal vigilance upon the devil race above him. On the many screens about him are magnified beam pictures of the several layers of the city above, those tiers of dwelling places filled with the life most dangerous to him.

The room is filled with "rapidity stim," an invigorating, conducive beneficial of such energy providing nature, so conducive of impulse that even his sleep is filled with complete awareness of all around him. To our way of thinking, the Messiah is one who does not sleep. He dare not sleep, but his mind has adopted the numerous types of physical support rays to his needs in such a way that his body is not tired by the necessity for constant watchfulness. (Some animals develop this unapproachable awareness, even while asleep).

The rapidity stim boosts his nerve command inpulses in such a way that his great body moves about the arsenal chambers with a speed that is to our eyes faster than vision. His hands are but blurs of motion on the myriad controls of the many great weapons.

Watching the thousands of devil people, watching their lancing, ever-attacking rays, killing them when opportunity presents, in continual warfare with men who command nearly as powerful weapons as himself, though with none of his vast command of the knowledge of their uses, or his understanding of the purpose the mechanisms were designed for, the Messiah has little time left for his original God-given plans—for the raising of force and following to attempt an enlightened rule of earth.

SO we see the Messiah, a flashing desperate whirl of motion, his hundreds of beams covering every part of the enemy city, his great, black form leaping from great screen to great screen, his blurring hands flashing bolt after bolt of flaming energy into the mass of defense rays which continually defend the devil ray's position. Occasionally his faster handling of the weapons gets through a deadly bolt and downs a dozen of the little devils that attack him. The battle of the forgotten deeps of the Holy Land goes on, week after week, and to those above on the surface nothing is noted of it— only a wonder in their hands as to why they are recently so free of the pestering deviltry of the invisibles who usually make their life a hell.

But the black Messiah found time to direct the young Jesus and his parents to a deserted city, as I told you. There he directed also certain wise men whom he had contacted before Jesus' birth. In this way he arranged for the education of Jesus, and we know how well Jesus was educated by his work. (By the scene in the temple where Jesus bested the wise old men of the temple priests although himself but ten).

The wonder of this man was not unnoted, and everywhere around the rea held by

Lila's father, Satantes Onderde, gathered slowing the rebels against his evil repression, and from afar from Egypt, from the Red Sea, from the northern lands of Greece and Italy, from under Rome itself, came ray men skilled and well equipped, and waited their chances to join forces with the mighty fighter who had been born of mother earth itself in the depths.

And even as the virgin birth of Jesus above was heralded as a wonder—so was the wonder of the birth of this terrible black man from the depths a miracle, and men came from the ends of the earth's depths to join themselves to him and to learn his mighty wisdom that was so great that he could fight against a whole kingdom of bloody and evil men and win day after day, and get up again and win again the next day—and kill an army of men and forget to sleep afterward.

The stories of the true Messiah were everywhere in the caverns. And the Messiah opened a way for these men who came bearing gifts and wisdom for him, and to learn, and swiftly his forces grew year by year. It was a strange and wild, yet a heartening scene, around him, the wild men of the north, from even Gaul, sitting side by side with a druid journeyed all the way from Brittany—crossing the Mediterranean by the great tunnel under Gibralter, and beside him sitting an Egyptian priest in his tall hat with the cleft, and beside the white robes of the Egyptian a near-naked black witch-doctor from Africa's dark jungles, and these repeated over and over into the hundreds, they say or took their turns at guard and at holding the way open for more and more to join the growing army that was learning every day the ancient logic that is wisdom. For young Yahveh did not teach "love," he taught "self-interest" and the logic of teaching other men to take care of each other that one may be taken care of—and the foolishness of treachery and evil intent that are taken up by other men if successful until the storm overwhelms one—and his words were like thtis: "And if a man is to make it rain, and has no roof, then he wets himself. And if a man raises up hate, then hate will consume him—and if a man teaches killing for gold, why he cannot possess gold or he will be slain and robbed. But if a man raises up love for one's fellows, and is a good hearty fellow, why if he teaches well men will love him for a good hearty fellow indeed. And if a man teaches other men to take care of the sick and tend them and make them well—why when he is sick they will tend him and make him well. But if a man teaches that selfishness says to rob the weak, and flatter the strong, and never to risk their neck against the strong for it is not wisdom—why when the bully sets upon him his friends will turn away, and he will face the bully alone. For the truly selfish man is the wise man, who treats his neighbor well, and greets the dusty traveler with food and wine—for he may wish to travel himself and that is wisdom to set an example to have people do those things. And when he is sick his neighbor brings him food." And with such simple images of proper conduct Yahveh built about himself a wise army of nomad seekers from the four wild quarters of the mysterious caverns. And among the men who came into his rays (power area) were sometimes spies sent by Satantes, the father of Lila, and Lila looked at them, and they went away—and Yahveh laughed. For she knew them.

And ten years went by.

And about him was a worshipping throng of men from afar, even black pigmies followed his words with wise nods and his movements with attentive eyes.

Daily did his trained fighters grow, and the small borders of his kingdom grew, and the holding of Satantes shrank before him, and Satantes' men died and fled, and presently Satantes picked himself and his few remaining followers up and went away and left "Yahveh the terrible" in sole undisputed possession of the caverns under

---

FOOTNOTE:—
This warfare of the caves, between the evil-intended ray people and the well-intended of the cavern life, still goes on today as it always has. All unobserved by the men of the surface, it has been waged fitfully, battles and massacres and long campaigns, and has since earliest times stalled off all the efforts to make of the ancient mechanisms a science for the use of the surface people. This deadlock, of such ancient duration, is due to the impregnable nature of the fortresses built by the Elder race about the cavern entrances and in other places deep in the rock. These entrances, few in the past, and now reduced to but a half score over all earth, have been held by evil. The Legendary contention of good and evil spirits.

FOOTNOTE:—
And the name of earth to them was Mi, and the name of the Messiah's mother Ma'ri, meaning earth as a mother, and the birth was the nature of him, he had not a father, but only the mystery of nature.

Jerusalem and for fifty miles around.

AND now Yahveh blasted out the thin shell of rock into a cleft between hills outside the city, and now some of the men he had been teaching from afar came to him from the city itself. And for a time all was well. And young Jesus grew.

Heretofore the Messiah had little time for his original plans, the raising of force and following for a great attempt at building an enlightened rule on earth. To make these foolish mortals wise and immortal again is the gigantic task set him by those who planted him there in the depths of the ancient cavern cities.

But now he had time for the teaching and hardening of leaders for his future armies, and he directed certain wise men to Jesus to teach him, and to many other men like Jesus he sent teachers in many places. And he taught them of the ancient past, of the writings that waited in the lost City and of himself, and Jesus thought of this unseen but terrifically helpful and ever watchful God as his Father.

Now there was this about the teaching of the young Jesus that finally frustrated all his use to the plans of the Messiah. The black giant in the depths knew that only a powerful organization ready to shed blood and use any pressure necessary and to fight fiercely and unremittingly for what they knew, was right, would win against the forces of evil. Whenever he tried to teach Jesus this, the watching Devil cut in with thought-tamper and told Jesus that such talk was "from the devil" and his men—that the way to win was to "turn the other cheek"—it is not wisdom to "create strife" even in defense of good.." And when Jesus did perceive the necessity for united and militant action and preached it—they nullified his efforts by tampering the thoughts of his followers into non-action. And all the time, in the far distance, their leader Satantes was gathering allies from other dero of the caverns, sending ambassadors to every ruler even into darkest Africa, even into Asia and into Europe, to call for help against the "Black Man" whose terrible wrath against evil was Satantes' best selling point, for evil was widespread, and the habits of the many rulers made them fear such righteous power with a great dread.

So against the Messiah was raised slowly and surely a terrible army of the witches from the north of the black magic witch-doctors from Africa, of the Men from Tibet, who hold that Yahveh was a false God who did not teach aright and must be fought for that reason, and from everywhere that a lie and a foolishness would be believed Satantes called forth strength and madness. And now slowly the ring of evil tightened on the work of the Messiah.

Now, the young God and the Christ child talked long hours every day, while the battle raged in a great circle all about the area.

When the young God appeared to Joseph and Mary in the great cave city, where they remained hidden for some ten years, it was as a "blaze of glory." A projection of his mighty being surrounded by the beams of massed beneficial ray generators and projectors he used to keep himself able to fight off the devil's ray tribe day and night.

Joseph and Mary and the wise men he had brought to teach Jesus fell down on their faces at sight of the projection,—in spite of their familiarity with it, the awe of his presence never failed to overcome them.

But the young Jesus always ran to the immaterial but solid-looking phantasm (the Holy Ghost) of the God, for the emanations of the rays were extremely pleasant and stimulating and the great God-man always greeted him like a father—so that Jesus called him "My Father, GOD !"

THE young God spent some time every day searching the mind of Jesus for erroneous ideas, ill intents, and putting in his day's need for new thought and for logical growth of new ways of thought. Then he outlined the morrow's work in teaching for the young Jesus to the men he had assigned to the work. The speaking apparation would then vanish, for he could not leave the ray screens but for short minutes, though these minutes added up to hours a day for the young child.

During such occupations Lila sat absorbed in watching the endless cone of distance that was the way to the south, the many openings marked with the little green lights that meant clean ray chambers with living equipment installed—with the soft good-for-the-eyes violet glow that was the ever-light of the caves, (put there to last endless lifetimes by the Gods before they knew the earth would be caught up by the sun's pull from its lonesome orbit in cold empty space). Everywhere in the distance that Lila watched for danger was the designed enigma of strong, mechanical beauty, the machine art that was titanic power of thought worked out into actual power machinery.

To Lila, this wonder of the past was just the every day landscape of life. But through this endless magic of comfort, through this paraphernalia of the life of Paradise itself, built for immortal living with all the means of life's support and life's infinite pleasures as the Gods themselves enjoy—inbuilt everywhere— through all this magic of the past of the Gods the naked feet of savages had whispered in the near past, —and the sandals of the Egyptian priesthood, and the black bearded, hook-nosed Assyrian secretives of the inner circles of their hierarchy had stolen in search of what wonders—and the Jewish ray—lords who resemble the Assyrian so much in face,—had lived and had degenerated in all that luxury into the Devil race that now flung its lightnings and its fury at the Messiah in futile efforts to remove the threat to their way of life—a way of life that left no way for other life at all.

And above all that flashing, deadly spite and wicked lancing fire, those flaming blue and yellow firebolt of doom, above all that fierce devilish anger and stupid Evil that stood between the race of man and man's future,—stood—towered,—dominated, the black and terrible figure that was the last God. Superior to all that death-dealing effort of the Devil race, dominating the whole 60 mile diameter circle of battle ray with his eye-blurring speed and endless understanding of what was needful to set at naught the efforts of the whole devil race, an Empire bent upon his death and thwarted by his lone efforts and his mastery of the terrifying ancient weapons. About him hurried the ignorant but clever-handed men of ray from the north, who hated these mad Jewish devil-ray. They had a kinder way of life, by heritage, and they had acquired from his teachings a worshipping desire to serve this man who brought to earth the ways of a life they knew had once existed here but was now lost from earth except for him—the way of the Gods had built their loved homes in the deep rocks and left the mysterious marvels that they could use but could not understand. Fight these devils who periled this new God who had come mysteriously to life here in these deeper caverns they could and did. It was an incongruous sight to see the sandled and white-robed men of Jerusalem focusing a gigantic ray screen side by side with a black, nearly nude Ethiopian,—and beside the Ethiopian a bearded priest of Isis, and beside him one of the Druids from Northern Gaul in dark woolen robes and rope sandals, his long black hair uncombed, his hairy thin legs bare and animal-like. And all of them fought well and again and again the tide of the devils was beaten back. But the men who came from afar to serve and to learn under the new Messiah of the deeps came in dribblets of strength, while the evil of Satanes Onderde was continually reinforced by groups of disciplined fighting men from other rulers who feared the wrath of the new Leader, Yahveh, the terrible.

One thing that wrung the heart of the young God was the fact that the great mansions, the beauiful cavern homes of his father, had been for centuries in the hands of savage vandals who had destroyed and effaced much of the artistic work, and had damaged beyond repair much of the invaluable mechanisms upon which healthy life in the caverns depended.

It was hard for the man-God to realize how very long a time had passed since his fathers, the Gods, had left Earth. The indestructible alloy of which they had built their machines and their furniture and decorated their homes, the doors, the water and drain pipes—were untouched by time. It was hard to realize by visible signs how long the passage of time, how vast the interval between their going and his birth.

Always his great mind fought with and wept over the waste of his time which the war with the devil ray-men necessitated. The largest part of his unsleeping hours were engaged in constantly shifting his defenses to meet some new weapon they had dragged from the endless reaches of the caverns to try out on him.

But the science of the Elder race living again in his great mind was too great a magic for their savage, unlettered and ignorant misuse of the mighty power of rav.

FOOTNOTE—From Rathsnothser's "Der Venushoehl" of 1473, from the Verholm trans. (page 82, par. 3).

"And within the Venushoehl is known to live not Venus or any other beneficent God or Goddess as of old legend had it, but Devils who destroy any who enter the opening. The peasants who live near fear them so greatly they will not approach within miles of the mount. This fear is so general that some 900 square miles of good farmland is uninhabited above the mount over the Venusshoehl. That something does live there still, something with powers such as legend has attributed to those who dwelt within the hollow mound centuries ago, is true! That "something," in spite of its powers, is no God—but some kind of fiend, for it but one-tenth of the deeds attributed to the hidden life be true, then the Devil himself has taken up abode in Venus' dwelling!"

(To be continued next issue)

READER'S SECTION

(Continued from page 5)

At the close of festivities, the members of the orchestra carrying instruments and cases to the waiting carriages, buggies, and horseless carriages, were aware that the drummer was not accompanying the others. A hurried search had revealed that he had walked through a pair of French doors and carrying, his bass drum only, had wandered off through the surrounding orange orchard. Being rather stubborn after a few drinks, he refused to return to the carriages with the others and it was decided to allow him to walk off his binge and knowing that he would obtain transportation, the others drove on to their respective homes.

That was the last that anyone, so far as is known, has ever seen of the man! He left a wife and family, friends, social position, a good living, etc. and just vanished. The law and private investigators could uncover no clues as to his whereabouts, nor as to his means of disappearance.

Apparently he entered the orchard, dressed in evening clothes, carrying a bass drum on his back, and never left the orchard!

Years passed and a friend loaned me a copy of Charles Fort's works and I read the book considering it a bit boring in its fantasy, having (what I considered) a scientific sort of mind, thought too far-fetched for serious thinkers. Suddenly I found myself excitedly reading Fort's account of the Australian party encamped in the vast desert of the interior of that continent. Into the light of their campfire about which the party was gathered, strode a white man, immaculately clad in evening clothes and carrying a bass drum on his back. He seemed not to be dusty nor tired. He showed no evidence of having walked more than a few yards through the wilderness. He could not tell how he happened to be there, how he arrived, nor did he know his own identity. He returned to civilization with the party and as I recall, Fort states that his identity was never established. Whether or not the man is alive, I do not know. I heard that the "widow" of the local musician who disappeared is somewhere in Phoenix, Arizona. I am making efforts to check on these two incidents. Teleportation?

In conclusion, let me state that I am using a psuedonym under which I have hopes of some day writing, having travelled in far-off lands, and having seen and heard many things which can only be explained by Shaverian theories.

Yours in the keen enjoyment that a Shaver Mystery brings to the human imagination. Hope that you publish this letter so that it may bring me ino contact with others interested in these phenomena . . . T. Arthur Ainslee, 508 S. El Monte Ave., Temple City, Calif.

Dear Mr. Ainslee:

I read the account in Fort too. I have often wanted to see an account of the origin of one of Fort's appearances. This strikes me as it!

There is a lot of corroboration for teleportation. I think they did it. The Elder race. If teleport mech stood around down there, these things would happen. These things do happen. Apparently this one was just done for the fun of noting a drunk's reaction to sobering up in Australia . . . but I guess this one forgot who he was as Fort mentions is common with these cases. That is easy to understand, as memory is so electric in nature the process would seem to remove it partially.

Have seen pictures of an old negro brought to caves via teleport—swoosh. The dero told him to climb on a bed of hot coals, as he was now in Hell. He did, he believed them. When he felt the pain, tried to get off, they pushed him back—looked like Hell legend repetition—did it start that way?—Shaver

* * *

Dear Mr. Shaver:

I think this is a fine thing, you and your associates have started. As much as I would like to believe those cave stories, I find myself incompatible. However, I do not consider that important. I do know however the source of the voice or voices. At the age of 21 years I experienced the first appearance of the "voices"—I am thirty now. The voices finally shaped up into one voice with varying characteristics. As a result of these voices I spent 18 months in a mental institution. During that time the voices were mostly chaotic and unintelligible. However I did learn a lot from that. Believe me. At the close of that period the voices began to shape up and became more rational. I slowly began to rely on the voice in my thinking. I find now that the voice is more intelligent than myself. I hear the voice almost constantly now. In fact I wouldn't be without it.

Now here is the only conclusion I can draw. I do not believe that any other conclusion can be drawn. In the construction of animal life we must become at some time one collective person literally. Instead of becoming independent beings we will become one and many. Mostly many, of course. Those voices were the embryonic manifestation of the interperson, depicted in mythology as the unicorn, as Christ, as Buddha, Allah, Hiawatha, and so forth. Or as the Jewish Torah would say, "The Kingdom of God is within you."

Now the elderly Brahmins go into hermitage to concentrate on being absorbed into Brahma. As they advance to the stage where the innerperson and themselves are blending. I am in that process now.

This Cave Club is no little thing. If of course we can advance in the process I have outlined cooperatively and scientifically we can make much faster progress. Also there is a chance that we can do it in a less brutal way than letting it just happen. You must have experienced much hardship yourself in the process. So leaving off the pretty words if I can save others from the tortures I went through, I will do it. You can see by this letter that I am no literary specialist. But if there is anything I can do in this process please let me know. I am convinced that you know what I have already said previously. Very sincerely yours . . . Beauford R. Telhitten, 3820 Avenue "M", Galveston, Texas.

* * *

Dear Mr. Shaver:

I remain interested in the Mystery, my attitude being, basically, "It's most unlikely, but not impossible and true or false the facts should be checked and published." I am a great believer in the wide dissemination of all facts, palatable and unpalatable, orthodox or not.

In this connection and in the spirit of honest inquiry, I would like to see published your answers to a few apparent contradictions which I have noticed published in your stories and articles in Amazing Stories.

Why, if the sun is so unhealthy and deadly, are those who grow up away from it, so unhealthy? This is common knowledge. Also, you mention in some of your stories, humans who have grown up in the caverns and are like "potato sprouts grown in a cellar." And for the same reason.

The original occupants of the caverns were supposed to be far in advance of us. Yet descriptions of their machinery are barely 50-100 years (if that) in advance of our present, scientifically possible, if not commercially attainable, knowledge.

I do not notice mention, any mention, of Atomic Power in any of those stories. Didn't they have it? If not, what did they use and why not atomic power? Are we (supposedly degenerate scientifically) ahead of them at any point? If so, how is it possible?

The builders of the caverns supposedly left ages ago because the sun would no longer support moral growth. Since that time it has become presumably worse. Yet, basically decent people are the rule rather than the exception. If your theory is correct, why isn't all humanity degenerate?

If the caverns exist, as you state, why haven't our extensive mines, (our immense gold, coal, silver, and iron mines, for instance) broken into them? Why hasn't our probing with radar, super-sonics, and similar instruments for geologic deposits, located them? Why don't they collapse as extensive abandoned mines do with similar disturbances on the surface?

I have not put these questions in a heckling spirit. I really want to know. If your story is correct then your answers to these should be logical. I would like to hear them. I have never been afraid of a fact merely because it was unorthodox: on the other hand neither do I swallow every ism that comes along.

At present, quite frankly, your story appears to me to be a hoax on the order of the Moon Hoax and the Cardiff Giant of a generation or so ago. However, I would be the first to admit my mistake if I found that I had been mislead by my own skepticism. All I ask is that the truth be found and that the proofs be published, either way, unmistakably and in heroic doses. As I mentioned in the beginning of this letter, I have a great fondness for truth, even if it makes my own face red! And if I can be of assistance other than financial (at present), I shall be glad to help. Please accept my apology for taking so much of your time. Very sincerely yours . . . Mrs. W. E. McCoy, Route 1, Box 609, Clatchanie, Oregon

Mrs. McCoy:

The sun still gives off exd, which is the base of growth. It is not entirely unhealthy. It is just that it causes age by throwing radioactives, too. We have to have it, or its equivalent. Yet the sun kills us, too.

The reason I can't give better descriptions of cavern mech, I don't know enough. Think of yourself telling an engineer of a space ship you had seen, when there are no space ships! I do my best. They were far beyond me, or any of us moderns.

All humanity IS degenerated . . . the ancient standard, was vastly higher. They were much more alive, and I wish I could tell you how they lived. For instance, when they camped out in the gigantic forests—they used a transparent teepee! Their whole life was terrifically different, richer, more pleasant in the extreme. Earth was just a whistle stop in a vast space system. Yet there were great things that brought many visitors to earth. I think they still do, but the visitors are not the same—they are from likewise degenerate planets. They come to see "The Great Tomb".

The caves are deeper than miners penetrate— and they are led away when they get too near. Mines get too dangerous—many mines are "haunted" no one will work in them.—Shaver

* * *

Dear Mr. Shaver:

May I ask if you'd check or have the club check on a theory of mine? This in line with the Shaver principles. As the Mystery has said these things:

1st: that growth in the "old days" was accelerated by the larger quantities of carbon ash given off by the sun at that time.

2nd: that since the time of "Sathanas" the amount of carbon ash has greatly decreased and is replaced by heavy metal-ash or de-energy.

3rd: that these factors have caused the human race to be unable to attain the true growth and longevity of which it is capable.

Therefore: I say that since the time aforementioned, the human race has standardized itself to a certain extent insofar as growth and longevity are concerned. But say for instance that in the last 200 years the sun has been burning increasing amounts of carbon gradually and in packets at certain times, or that the element next above carbon in the atomic scale has been transmuted by the sun's energy in greater amount these last centuries into carbon and then burning that into carbon ash.

Possibly the first result of this kind of an occurrence or increased ability to use our intelligence as is indicated by the scientific achievements of the past century.

But what of the effect on the human body? I'd say that carbon ash in small amounts proportionate to the needs of the standardized people in this respect of absorption of it, would spread over the whole body wherever carbon is needed for normal growth. But increasing or varying amounts over our needs would cause it to be stored in the place of carbon in fat or as sugar in the liver.

As this ash is a growth factor capable of producing enormous growth a blind man can see what might happen because of an accumulation of this substance—cancer!

As I know it, cancer is an enlargement or growth of an area of cells in a portion of the body to the detriment of the rest of the body.

Please in some way let me know what you or the club thinks of the theory as I'm vitally interested. My Mother has it and will not live very long on that account. If you agree with me, perhaps you'd pass it on to others of the Shaver Fans and to the Medical public. Yours respectfully . . . Gail Harvey, 960 Huron St., Racine, Wisconsin

Dear Gail Harvey:

I agree with you in your analyses.

About your mother, I suggest you try to get ray-people to help her. They could, if they wanted to. They often want to, there is too much for the ones so inclined to tend to.

You can get this help by thinking very intensely about your need in the quiet night —and they may be able to tend to it. A penetray will examine the C. and a needle will kill it and the roots. She won't even feel it.

Try it. But don't expect anyone to believe what did it. The doctors will call it a . . . big word, meaning miraculous disappearance of a malignant growth. Your friend,

Shaver.
                                        *   *   *

Dear Mr. Shaver:
    I too believe there is more truth than fiction in the Shaver stories. I have my bit to contribute for what it is worth. I have just finished the June issue of the Shaver Mystery. In the Discussions there is a letter from Mr. Marx Kaye. Mr. Kaye states that a few years ago in Los Angeles, Cal. he witnessed one evening, an object in the sky, said object followed by a trail of fire, etc.
    He also said he had no witnesses. But I believe I saw the same thing. As I remember, it was in Sept. of 1944 or 1945. My husband and I were returning from a late movie. The time was about eleven P.M. We were walking. It was one of those clear balmy evenings that only southern California can have. We were just strolling along enjoying the night when we were startled by a brilliant light that seemed to light the whole city. Looking up we saw a long object of fire. There was a loud hissing and sputtering and a long trail of sparks tailing behind.
    The ship (?) or whatever it was came out of the North and flew (?) or at any rate disappeared into the Northwest.
    It was flying (?) in a horizontal position. When it reached the center of the city there was an explosion as of the back-firing of a car, only many times louder accompanied by a fresh shower of sparks and fire. When this occured, the ship(?) changed course from North to South to Northwest and disappeared. We, at the time, in our ignorance, assumed it to be a comet or a meteor. But, whoever saw either fall horizontally or change course?
    Never the less we watched the papers for several days to see if the observatories reported any comets or meteors. But we failed to find it in any paper. This may mean nothing to you and then again it may be another link in the Mystery. I sincerely hope so. I have experienced a few other odd incidents that I will not write about today. But I will have them for another time. In all sincerity, I remain . . . Mrs. Cleo Helmann, Box 262, Richardton, North Dakota.

Dear Mrs. Cleo Helmann:
    We have a large number of such reports as your own. They all indicate that space ships do visit earth—but why and what they do are mysteries.
    We think that many people know this and have commerce with the caravan and with the space ships—that we are left out of it all. We are kicking . . . Hence the Shaver Mystery.—Shaver

                                        *   *   *

Dear Mr. Shaver:
    I have read every story that you have written for Amazing and Fantastic Stories from "I Remember Lemuria" down to the present time and the only way that I can express my appreciation of them is just to say that I think they're TOPS!
    The only kick that I have to make is that things just don't move fast enough. I would like to tell you about a friend of mine. His name is C. J. Spillman. I met him when he was racking pool balls in a local billiard parlor. As a joke a friend of mine told me to ask him if I could read his manuscripts. The joke was on me. He did. Here is an outline of his "story" and some of the pertinent facts that he told me which were not mentioned in the "story."
    Mr. Spillman wrote this story at the insistence of a friend. It was never intended to be published but was just for the entertainment of his friend. In 1912 Mr. Spillman was asked to make a trip to South America with two friends of his. One of his friends whom we shall call "Mr. Jones" recently had come into an inheritance from his grandfather. His making this trip was a stipulation in the will. After arriving in San Simon (I believe this was the name of the town), Bolivia, they left civilization. After many days travel they arrived at a place which looked as if it had been bombed. After looking around through the jumble of rocks, they found an opening to a small cave. Inside a little ways the cave gradually got larger until it was large enough to walk around in, comfortably. For the space of about three days, the three walked down and ever down. At the end of this time they came into a cavern which was so large they could not see the other side of it. Coming toward them were three men who were about eight feet tall and who looked exactly alike. They looked like Christ must have looked because of the look of peace and serenity on their faces and their long flowing white hair. These men took them to their city and made them welcome.
    Facts about them: they were all males. They were all vegetarians. They thought

it cannibalistic to eat meat. They reproduced artificially. They were an exploration party from another planet. They said Christ was just a man far ahead of his time in knowledge. They lived for three hundred years but did not die but ascended like Christ did.

Mr. Shaver, I could go on for three or four pages telling you about Mr. Spillman's manuscript but I won't. I just wanted you to get some idea of what it's like because Mr. Spillman is just as sincere as you are when he said he *had* this adventure.

Now, Mr. Shaver, I'm going to start haranging you. That's no news, but there are a few things I want you to know. Do the people in the caves need help? And if they do, how can we help them? Do they need men to fight? How can a person get to the caves? Are the caves up or down?

I am quoting this from your article "Voices In The Night" in the Shaver Mystery Club Magazine. Quote: Voices in the night say; Tell 'em outright, get 'em down here, we need 'em plenty! Mr. Shaver, please, if they need help, let's give it to them. There must be plenty of men who believe in you and who are willing to go with you.

I am 24 years old and a fireman for the Southern Pacific Railroad, but right now I am laying off and going to radio school. I have been studying radio for three years. I have a private pilot's license and used to own my own plane. I am a high school graduate, weight 185 pounds, am six feet tall and am considered very healthy. Yes, I'm a veteran too; I have worked at most everything; mined coal, worked in the shipyards, aircraft plants, copper smelters, railroads and know the Western United States exceptionally well.

The reason I'm telling you these things, Mr. Shaver, is that I'm willing anytime to go along to the caves with you and fight like the very devil.

So long for now Mr. Shaver. Sincerely . . . Wayne D. Simpson, 1708 W. Madison St., Phoenix, Arizona

Dear Wayne:

Wish I could tell you how to help them. They are dominated by a selfish luxurious clique who are robbing us all of the most needed science knowledge on earth. They don't have much use for it or men either. They live for pleasure. There are only a few places you could enter the caves, and most of those would lead you into the wrong hands. You would be a needless sacrifice. Where to find the leaders of the other side, the ones who fight for us and the underdogs in the caverns, I don't know. Try and find them is all I can say. I don't even know how to try. How would you find capitalist sympathizers in Russia, say?

When they are ready they will tell us—till then, I guess we wait and hope. That has been going on for a good many centuries—and we are still not even knowing of the Elder world.

Note for your deduction—Governor Green's ceiling fell in the day after he refused to refund a lot of tax money to Chicago. Does that tell you anything? He always takes a nap there, had just stepped out—Shaver.

* * *

Dear Mr. Shaver:

I have just received the first issue of your magazine today in the mail; "The Shaver Mystery Magazine" and a copy of "Science Comics" and I can honestly say that your magazine lived up to more than I thought it ever would. I expected to get a mimeographed 3 or 4 pages of not too impressive material. But you presented in your mag much interesting information which I often wondered about pertaining to the mystery. Once again I say, good work on your first issue; keep it up. Yours sincerely—Jack Hart, 404 Linden Road, Birmingham, Michigan

Dear Jack:

You'll get your copy at your new address. The mag will be even bigger when we can get paper for it. Mandark gets much better, too. There will be other writers, other articles—and a bigger letter section. But it takes time, and printing and paper conditions are the worst possible.—Shaver

* * *

Dear Mr. Shaver:

If the Chinese came from the moon, as some of their legends say they do, the following is a theoretical account of how it could have happened.

According to the Volume Library's historical section the mariner's compass was known to the Chinese in 1115 B.C. Therefore, it is probably safe to assume that they understood magnetism and, by extension, gravity.

It is thought, by some scholars, that gunpowder was known by the Chinese and used by them in the form of firecrackers in their religious festivals at least a thousand years before Roger Bacon discovered it in 1247.

The escape velocity from the gravity of the earth is seven miles per second. The moon's escape velocity is about one sixth that of the earth or about one and one sixth miles per second. Soon after leaving the moon's surface a rocket ship would enter the earth's gravity field and would be attracted to the earth for the greater part of its journey. Once free of the moon's gravity no more power need be applied, letting the rocket coast to the earth until it became necessary to brake the ship's fall to the surface.

Physics tells us that if an object at a height of sixteen feet above the earth were set in motion at 4.9 miles per second it would encircle the earth forever since its velocity at that height would neutralize earth's gravity.

Gunpowder would be the fuel for their rocket motors and thereby their means of leaving the moon and the means of slowing their ship on its arrival at earth.

The Chinese scientists might have been able to figure a way for their ship to become a satellite of earth, perhaps at a thousand miles above the earth's surface. By so doing they could avoid the direct attraction of earth's gravity which would result in a considerable saving of fuel. That is to say, that by becoming a satellite of earth by encircling it at 4.9 mps instead of directly repelling the attraction all the way at 7 mps, it would cut the power necessary to repel earth's gravity by 25%.

Their are several ways in which the people on such a ship could finally land on earth. 1) By alternately lowering and raising the ship's 4.9 mps speed to let it circle lower and lower until it landed. 2) By sending small shuttle ships to earth.

Probably you are wondering what all this has to do with the Shaver mystery. Theoretically it proves: 1) People do exist on other planets as Shaver says. 2) Rocket travel is possible between planets. 3) To my way of thinking it answers one of anthropology's biggest questions—the race of man. I don't hold with some scientist's opinion that the entire human race came from Central Asia. I offer the foregoing theoretical account of how the Mongolian race came to this earth.

If it can be *actually* proved that at least one of the races of man did not originate on this world but came from another planet, then the Shaver mystery will certainly be proved in at least one way—that other worlds besides this one are inhabited by human beings. Sincerely yours . . . James R. Guyton Jr., 1933 Middle St., Sharpsburg, Pa.

Dear Mr. Guyton:
I have heard there are in Smithsonian some ancient Chinese wet cell batterys—so they had electrical knowledge too!

But I don't think they came here with gunpowder. I think they came during the period the caverns were known on the surface of earth—in the ancient space ships that still lie down there unused—and mostly unusable now.

Since that day, the knowledge of the caverns has been lost to surface man—and that was not an accident . :. Shaver

*   *   *

Dear Mr. Shaver:
Just received my magazine. I think it one of the nicest ones I've ever had . . . I haven't had time to read it all . . . but . . . it's WORTH 50c per copy. I most certainly DON'T want to miss even ONE copy so please drop me a card and let me know if you are taking full year subscriptions . . . or only for every two months.

I personally know of two caves . . . one in Mass. and one in upper N. Y. I intend to visit the one in Mass. this summer. Mr. Shaver asked that I send him a piece of the jewelry supposedly made by the owner of the property . . . which I will do when I go to visit the cave. In the two attempts I've made to enter the caves in Mass. (one has to go down a ladder to get to the main hall as it is far below ground) I've FAINTED . . . yet I'm NOT . . . as a rule the FAINTING KIND! BUT . . . I will get down someway THIS time and will describe . . . even take snaps if possible . . . and buy some of the pieces of jewelry to send Mr. Shaver.

Again . . . thanks for a really GRAND magazine. Sincerely . . . Ginger Zwick, Just-A-Mere-Farm, Orchard Park, New York

Dear Ginger:
You will like the magazine much better when you really get into Mandark and when we get enough paper to make it bigger as we planned.

Please do get hold of at least photos of that man and his jewelry and his story. If it's really the old stuff, you will get a life-time subscription to Amazing and a few

other tokens of my appreciation. The real value . . . ! of it? . . . Shaver

* * *

Dear Mr. Shaver:

Enclosed are some notes, observations that I have noticed in my time. Probably you know all this data and much more.

There is no doubt that caves and tunnels do exist underground, but to my knowledge I have never met a ghost, goblin, troll, dero or another of your fascinating friends . . . I doubt if they really do exist and if they do I am not anxious to make their acquaintance anyway . . .

In my travels around New York and New England I have come into contact with stories of caves and the so-called 'bottomless' holes . . . which, as I understand your theory, really do go down to the ancient layers . . . In talking with a number of well-educated country people they never mention any supernatural stuff, but do know that fish and some forms of wild life do travel underground rivers, their disinterest in these matters seem to be based on the fact that such exploration is unprofitable and having some knowledge of geology do not think these 'holes' will lead to anything worthwhile in minerals or other things of value.

Anyway you do have a fascinating 'line' and I like to read it . . . Sincerely yours . . . T. J. Owen, Ph.C., 2951 Decatur Avenue, New York 58, New York

OBSERVATIONS

My grandfather Colonel J. C. Owen, soldier and engineer often mentioned odd things to me. He was a Puritan of the 'Old School' matter of fact, honest, and not at all imaginative, he seemed to *know* a lot of things and how he knew or learned I do not know. I do know he was usually right and never questioned his judgment or do so now.

One thing he mentioned about Manhattan . . . the island stands on a rock, but he states that the rock 'stands quaker' ie a V formation with the V point downward . . . also that the rock has a fault or split at least ⅔ of the way from the Battery up-town . . . I asked if he thought it of danger and his opinion was 'as long as the mass removed for building will exceed the weight of the buildings . . . no . . . but that an earthquake or severe shock might in the future split the rock' . . .

Lake 'Westchester' under the upper part of Westchester Co. and Southern Putnam and western Fairfield Co. is a huge lake not tapped at present . . . wells driven there only go to sub-surface water . . .

That submarine channels exist between the Finger lakes in upper New York . . .

Die Hexenschusse many of my older German speaking patients refer to a sudden stab of pain to a 'Hexen Schusse' ie a 'Witches shot' . . . this of course when the pain has no really apparent cause . . . of course the Chiropractic theory of the sub-luxation explains these pains and also the Chiropractic adjustment removes them . . . of course this is a figure of speech from earlier and more ignorant days.

While on duty with the U.S. Army at Pine Camp, N. Y., I noticed hills, mostly sandy that looked like the truncated pyramids of Mexico . . . also reef of rock that looked like walls . . . well laid but without cement . . . these seemed too perfect to be natural . . . I contacted the N. Y. State Dept. of Geology but was advised that these were odd natural formations found in that region and commented on by others who had mistaken them for ancient ruins . . .

I have heard that in that area are some Mound Builders 'forts' but have never seen them . . .

I do know of the Derset in Maine and its peculiar sands, also of the 'unexplored' forest some 200 miles in area as I was told but know nothing concrete here either . . .

I did while in the Army see the famous ore pit on Iron Mountain, near Peekskill, N. Y., and when we dropped pebbles down it was 40 seconds before we heard a splash . . . this is a early Colonial mine and while we talked a bit of further exploring naturally nothing came of it as it is located on a Military Reservation (Camp Smith) and saw it while there on duty with the N.Y.N.G. Naturally the Army doesn't encourage soldiers in much exploring of this type of place and it would of course be only for experienced men with good equipment . . .

Between Peekskill and Lake Mohecian, N. Y., is Gregorys Pond . . . it's a place that even the natives tend to shun . . . said to be 'bottomless' but really *a big* silt hole . . . fish there are full of silt . . . so the natives avoid it . . . saw an odd shark-like type of fish taken from there when a child . . .

Crumhorn Lake . . . near Cooperstown, N. Y. on top of a mountain, no inlet or outlet . . . also 'bottomless' . . . good fishing . . .

While on duty with the N.Y.N.G. at Camp Smith, N. Y. during the Summer of 1937 a group of us were listening to the Band Concert on the Parade Ground shortly after dark.

Suddenly a huge meteor slid slowly across the sky . . . it was bright red in color, coming in from the northeast . . . it crossed way above us but seemed to move slowly and disappeared in the hills across the Hudson. At that time I was a non-com in H.Q. Co. duty and my pal Sgt. Mullholland, a very matter of fact chap, said lets amble over to the Adjutant's Office where we worked. His idea was that if it hit anywhere near us we might have to get out men to fight a forest fire if it hit anywhere near enough. At Taps we called State Police H.Q. for the usual routine checkup but they said nothing about the meteor nor did we . . . anyway we felt a bit foolish about the whole thing and promptly forgot the whole thing . . .

It has been called to my attention that there have been an unusual number of cancer cases among men who were in the S.W. Pacific area during the war . . . maybe due to too much sun . . . irriadation? . . .

Dear Doctor Owen:

Read your observations with interest. Want to say that Die Hexenschusse was better understood in the old days than today—when we know so much we overlook the true from the past. The Witches still do it to us, but we explain it away. Did you ever read Cotton Mather's account of his trials? There are some interesting accounts of Witch trials in Scotland and England, too.

Glad you like my yarns. Only wish I could really picture the Elder race as it was. Twenty feet tall, eggs nine to a bushel—earth was different then! Beowulf mentions the building of the giant race under earth—other old writings do almost invariably include some mention.

Got a clip yesterday from Wash. about pilot seeing nine saucers traveling at 1200 miles an hour at ten thousand feet. He had instruments, telescope—looking for a wrecked transport. Wish I could get to the bottom of some of the space ship reports, too. Seems a lot of them are round or disc shaped . . . Shaver

* * *

Dear Mr. Shaver:

I hate to complain about your Shaver Mystery Magazine right at it's birth, but I feel it is my duty. When I first glanced at your magazine, my first thought was that my name must have been placed on the subscription list of a nudist colony publication by mistake. If you don't know what I mean (But I am sure you do) I am referring to the Illustrations.

Can't you guys realize that such pictures have no place in a magazine that calls itself scientific? Are you so money-mad that you would sacrifice the respectful appearance of your magazine just so you could get the additional customers who would buy it for the illustrations only?

But, Hark! Perhaps it is the work of a fiendeshly clever dero attempting to discredit your mag, eh? But still, you are only counter-acting your "efforts" to raise the moral standards of the human race. There are a lot of subjects you can base your illustrations on besides those you now use. Why not print a few photographs that you might have? Yours Truly . . . Thomas A. Smith, Fuquay Springs, Route 1, N. C.

Dear Mr. Smith:

The Elder race didn't believe in clothes, went nude a great deal. Besides artists like to paint 'em, and people like to look at them. Where would we be if people were born with clothes on? I ask you!

Sin is in the eye of the beholder, God said to Adam and Eve, and when they started wearing leaves around their middle, he threw them out of the Garden of Eden. He was right!

Elder race teachings are the same. Clothes are worn because of a de-infected mind which feels shame because of de charges on the body which affect the mind and the eye causing a mental sensation which seems to be thought but is not—a feeling of shame and sin—and when connected with sex—it is a bad thing for the human race.

I like modern art better than Byzantine—and they wore clothes up to the chin. They were wrong. Sin is in the mind, not on the skin . . . Shaver.

* * *

Dear Mr. Shaver:

In the first Shaver Mystery Mag. on the last page in "Letters From Readers," I read a letter from "Henry West" of 138 Lincoln St., Midvale, Utah. This chap's experience is similar to one I had with my first husband.

To set the scene I must first tell you that we were living at a gold mine in the Organ Mts. in New Mexico about sixty miles or more northwest of Elpaso, Texas. My husband was top-ground Engineer and I was State Bookkeeper.

Often on Sundays we would get in our eight cyl. Stude. and with our wolf-hound leave "The Bean Blossom" mine, I believe they called it and go exploring on our own.

Far up on the scarred Mt. we noticed signs of an old abandoned Mine. We parked the car at it's base and with only a 22 rifle and our wolf-dog, started to climb the ore-splattered Mt. side. Arriving at the Mine's entrance we entered a large room in which early miners had evidently lived, for old stoves, broken beds and empty cans littered the space.

At the rear a great iron fire-door gaped open. We walked through into an immense, throne-like room where the ceiling and near-by walls sparkled with "fools-gold and copper hues."

Deciding to explore further, we built a huge fire from old boxes and crates found in the once lived front room. We lighted pine slabs and re-entered the Mine. We walked a great distance until looking back, our bond-fire became a small torch of distance.

We had taken the left side of the mine on going in. We decided to get out of there and finally turned right and started back. My husband led the way and soon outdistanced me. My pine torch was flickering out so I called to him. He yelled back to keep coming in a straight line. I could see his pine torch bobbing far ahead of me.

I reached out my left hand, still holding my dimming torch and felt empty space. That didn't startle me at the time. Then, my right hand encountered hard rock, a wall-like structure. I kept my right hand on it and stumbled on. Finally, I threw away my now glowing embered torch and as I did so, I saw it go down, down until the glowing ember was swallowed up by darkness. I stood perfectly still. I was afraid to go on and I was afraid to stay. I hadn't heard that torch hit anything. I got down on my gabar-dined jodpured knees and crawled keeping my right shoulder brushing that rock wall. Finally I drew near the lighted entrance where our bonfire was throwing its beams. I got up and ran to my husband and told him about the incident. Naturally man-like(??) he pooh-poohed the idea and said he'd show me I was wrong.

This time we took an armful of lighted fagots and as we neared the spot where we had walked and I had later crawled on a narrow ledge about eighteen inches wide. To the left of the ledge was this immense hole. It gaped inky-black. We dropped and rolled rocks into space and no noise came up. My husband's face was a pasty white when we reached our bonfire.

Back at our own Mine we told an old sour-dough about it. First he bawled H— out of us and then he told us the great hole was known as a "Glory-Hole." Miners avoided those places and that accounted for that rock wall. The Miners had left it standing between them and the immense Glory Hole.

Now where do you suppose this great cavity leads to? This happened in 1932. Could it connect with Carlsbad Cavern? That has never been fully explored. "Glory-Hole" must mean that if one stepped into it one would go to "Glory."

Another strange thing has happened to me, twice in the past year. A very warm something has hit my feet coming through my shoe soles. This has happened in the same spot in my little living room. This very warm sensation streaked like lightning toward my knees then died out.

I very foolishly told a friend and she rather insultingly told me, (don't laugh now) that it was probably some change taking place in me. First I'm too young and second, I asked a Doctor and after his diagnosis he told me, "NO." So where did that very warm sensation come from through my shoe soles? No, I'm not over a furnace and I'm on the third floor, with no radiators near that spot.

Thanks for the letter of explanation and the interesting Mag. Sincerely . . . Helen Compton Gordon, 6334 Ingleside Ave., Chicago 37, Ill.

Dear Mrs. Gordon:

Nearly everyone, if they tell the truth carefully, has had similar experiences to the heat ray on your feet. If you read Chas. Fort's books, you would find cases of dozens of people who burn up, without even scorching their clothes! But don't worry, it is just an inquisitive ? taking a look. Usually a child, the older ones would not betray their presence, being more skilful.

About the Glory Hole, we have dozens of these to look into—if we could. Some of them with weird phenomena . . . For instance the place where Tannhauser courted Venus is still waiting in Germany, called the Venusbeurg—the Hollow Hill of the opera. No one will live near it because of the devilish things that happen. It is supposed to be the abode of Devils.

Hope you will stick with the Mystery till we really get to the bottom of some of these Glory holes . . . Shaver

* * *

Dear Mr. Shaver:

I have just finished reading the June issue of "Amazing Stories" and the additional proof that was offered in connection with the "Shaver Mystery." I have also received your letter in connection with the formation of the Shaver Mystery Club.

Having read all of the Shaver stories concerning the caves and the underground people, I feel that it is entertaining fiction but with no foundation in fact. Here in West Virginia we have numerous caves, some of them reaching thousands of feet underground, as well as numerous deep coal mine shafts which have been explored, and nothing has ever been found to indicate that such things exist as Shaver claims, in the underground. We also have an active organization of the Speleological Society who have done considerable exploring of the state's very many caves, and to date no artifacts or anything of an unusual nature have been discovered.

It is rather odd in the extreme that the Rosicrucian Order of which I have been a member for a good many years, makes no mention in any of their writings ancient or modern about cavern dwellers; since this organization goes in for research in such matters, it is indeed strange that if such things exist underground that the Order has not noted the fact in its many avenues of research. Some years ago it was brought to the Order's attention that a mysterious band of people, were living near Mt. Shasta in California. It was promptly investigated but no definite proof was established.

As to the Atlans fleeing to another sun, I view this statement with a great deal of skepticism. The chances that they found another star more suited to their habitat is indeed remote. There are few if any stars like our sun, most stars are larger and hotter, and many of the smaller ones differ greatly in physical makeup from our sun, indeed latest astronomical research is of the opinion that our sun is the only one that has a retinue of planets.

I can agree with Shaver on one particular, at one time in the past there was a race of giant people who according to measurements made on certain skeletons found in certain parts of the world, measured between 16 and 18 feet in height, also certain skeletons of the Mound Builders revealed the fact that some of them were 8 or 9 feet tall. Whether they were true men, or not has never been definitely established.

In regard to Shaver's Theory of immortal life, this is an impossibility. Nothing in nature has immortal life, it is a law of nature that all thngs die in the usual cycle of things.

If as stated in "Amazing Stories" we were visited by space ships, these could have come only from our solar system, there is a possibility that this could happen. Inhabitants of Mars or Venus might reach us as these are the only two worlds that would be capable of supporting life as we know it.

From some reading and research I have done, it is my opinion that we can accept the existence of Atlantis and Lemuria with some limitations. One was in the Atlantic Ocean, one in the Pacific, but the people were much the same as we are today, in many respects they advanced along scientific lines, and when Atlantis was overwhelmed, the survivors sought homes in other places. A group of them settled in Egypt. Finding that their race was about to die out, they erected the great pyramid of Egypt with its message to future man. Facts point to this as the later Egyptians looked with as much astonishment on the great pyramid as we do today. The Egyptians of 3000 years B.C. were not very far advanced, and whoever erected the pyramid had a profound knowledge of Georgraphy, Mathematics, and Engineering as well as Astronomy.

In conclusion I would say that Mr. Shaver does much better work in such stories as "Loot of Babylon" instead of the idea that we are threatened by cavern dwellers. A race that can invent an atomic bomb has little to fear from them. A bomb dropped in a cavern and—Whoosh, No dero, No mech, no telaug—No. Nothing! Sincerely yours . . . H. R. Wickline, A.B., A.M., Box 525, Logan, West Virginia.

H. R. Wickline:

Dear Sir,

Would call to your attention the book "Unveiled Mysteries" by Godfrey Ray King.

Also, I myself had telepathic communication with Rosicrucian Teachers, as well as face to face. That they do not mention the caverns IS VERY STRANGE to me too. Certainly they must "no" plenty about them.

Ray King describes a "spirit" trip through the whole underworld and some more, and it is in the most Occult phraseology, so perhaps you will enjoy it. Do not know what connection Saint Germain Press has with Ros. but Occultists do talk of caverns at length . . . Shaver.

PS   The cavern dwellers are the only people on earth who are at present safe from the atom bomb. I wouldn't suggest anything to them.

* * *

Dear Mr. Shaver:

Unfortunately or fortunately I am one of the numerous persons who have never heard an immaterial projection of a voice that they can remember except as in a dream picture. That statement I cannot swear to as being the absolute truth. The answer is simply I do not know what would be the truth about certain dream pictures. These outstanding thoughts or pictures have occurred to me at various times.

One I had in Summer in the year, 1945, at Camp Carson, Colorado where I was working as a clerk in the army administration units. The impression I received was out of the usual happenings of the day. I suddenly felt a strange sensation steal over me, and I closed my eyes. In some fashion I saw or felt that something far out in space (nearly to Pluto) was doing something, and then they swung out again into outer space. I saw or felt the darkness and coldness of that region out there.

Another case was when I was small, I had dreams of certain type that recurred over and over again. This was a dream in which people were torturing a man, or they were traveling somewhere. These two impressions occurred many times and did not cease until we moved from Eastern Oregon to Western Washington for short stay there. The travel business always puzzled me. If I had dreams of a trip I had made in a car, we started and we arrived somewhere. But these other instances we started somewhere and traveled to an unknown destination. It was always dark or it was grey or brownish light that was shed over the scene. I never recognized any of the passing landmarks as I gazed through a window in the traveling vehicle. That window was always to the front. I think I never saw a side window as long as these dreams occurred.

As for the torture, as far as I could ever see in the dream, the victim never died or wasn't allowed to die. Hot irons, tar, boiling liquid like oil were used on the victim who was bound to some kind of bench or framework. Always there was the queer half-light, grey or brown tone cast, shed over the scene.

I began seeing these dreams when I was six years old and they continued until I was twelve and half years old. At this time we moved away. At first I was afraid but later on became very curious about the whole thing. When after a severe illness, I couldn't go back to school for a year and I did a fair amount of research on certain subjects. In the academic textbooks and books I couldn't find the answers.

While I was in Colorado during the war, I heard some interesting stories about Pike's Peak which was seven or nine miles from our camp. One old timer told me about hearing falls of rocks that seemed to be inside the mountain. Geologists have heard these rock falls and seem to think the mountain had hollow spots or cavern in it. I had several others tell me about hearing rocks falling as if underground.

The country has a layer of limestone running under a lava cap and other softer stone. I had went through one small cave in the area. This cavern was nearly on top of a high hill. We went down some three hundred before we climbed back up to the upper entrance. Parts of this cavern have not been opened to the public and some may not even be explored as of yet. As they make enough funds, they explore and open up the sections of the cave. They say there are other caves in the area but none have been found that are large enough to warrant consideration . . . Howard F. Griffin, Oregon State College, Corvallis, Oregon.

Dear Mr. Griffin:

I would say your dreams were accidental telepathic contact with cavern people's minds. This happens so frequently because they use augmentation of thought, and the thought can be heard for miles when augmented. Many mech do this without there being any help for it—for instance a ray reaching out into space to search a space ship augments the occupants thought to make it readable. You would hear this even above ground if you happened to have even slight telepathic powers. You must know these exist in some people more than others if you ever heard of E.S.P. experiments. It has been proven over and over that E.S.P. is a fact, a fact that varies with individuals. (Extra-sensory-powers perception)

In torture they augment the victim's mind to fully enjoy his torment. In travel, they must pass search rays which augment their thought to betray their intents— enemies or friends . . . Shaver

*   *   *

Dear Mr. Shaver:

If we are to accept your revelations as authentic, we must make allowances, and be prepared to face these quirks of human nature, of which the chief is the innate desire to dominate, by either power, or money, our fellow men. I fear that we must examine carefully all who seek to enter upon, and to study, the secrets of the Caves, especially the more portable weapons, and other devices that could be easily used by ruthless men to enslave the rest of mankind.

There is an evident contradiction in the first issue of The Shaver Mystery Magazine regarding entrance and study of the caves—on page 14: the last paragraph before the Foreword to "Mandark"—Shaver says—"It takes years of contact to remove the fear and to make of a surface man a ready friend, or servant. Too, their customs are such that a person entering would be the next thing to a slave"—on page 35: third paragraph —Shaver says—"Other nations are down there, Yugo-Slavia, Ex-Nazis, French, English, Portugese. They are all hard at work, moving the wonderful mech to caverns under their countries, and laughing at the "modern" Americans, who are so modern that they cannot believe in the Elder races"—*NOW:*

HOW DID THE OTHER NATIONS GET DOWN THERE WITHOUT BEING ENSLAVED?

HOW DID THEY GET PAST THE "WATCHERS" (Page 11—Nydia's Words P.P. 2.)?

WHY DOES SHAVER INSIST IN SOME PLACES THAT NO OUTSIDER WOULD BE WELCOMED, AND IN OTHERS PRACTICALLY BEG FOR THEM TO COME?

IF the remnants of the Elder Race do actually reside in the Caves, and have the Mind reading machinery, and Mental Compulsion Mech that Shaver describes—WHY DON'T THEY USE IT TO TUTOR SURFACE PEOPLE?

IF they really want the help that Shaver almost begs for on Pages 35 to 37, *WHY* can't they determine who is infected by "de" to prevent the misuse of their potent mech by the surface people? When given to us.

IF they have Telesolidograph projectors, why are they always used to contact individuals? And not assembled groups?

Would Shaver actually have us believe that the massed minds of "de infected" man are actually stronger than the antique mech he describes?

IF Shaver has actually handled the antique mech—why can't he describe it in technical language, or provide schematic diagrams, instead of using a mess of terms that no one could possibly salvage any meaning out of—can he draw actual picturizations of such devices, clear enough to show some of the operating principles?

Sincerely hoping that you can use this letter, and that maybe you can get some answers to the above questions, I remain—Sincerely yours . . . Milton C. Erland, 3900 Spuyten Duyvel Parkway, Riverdale, New York City 63, New York.

Dear Erland:

The report that other nations than our own are down moving away the machines is only a report, and may be a lie. I heard, I don't necessarily believe it. Neither does it mean nations as governments, but as groups, secretive too—who have long had contact. It seems to me that there are more aliens down there than people from our own Modern USA. The machines are ripped out and taken away—some to space ships, some to under other countrys. They do laugh at us for being fools about it.

They passed the "watchers" because they either bribe them, kill them, or work for them.

There are many groups, some of them do recruit from the surface, in others enslave. Still others allow no contact with the surface.

There are no remnants of the Elder race alive. There are some bodies preserved in amber plastic, they were over twenty feet high. Some of the last of them were killed by some cataclysm, apparently a heat wave, but it could as well have been a flood.

Could you describe and diagram a Martian mechanism? Neither can I fully describe or technically understand Elder mech. They used flows that were not electric—not electrons. What were they? Some were same as flows in our nerves. Is that really electric? Crile says it is. Read him . . . Shaver

* * *

Dear Mr. Shaver:

I have received the magazine and, safe it is to say, I did not lay it down until I had read it from cover to cover. I am so glad to be a ground floor member of the club. It seems to me I can see where Mr. Shaver is trying so hard to tell the people of this country a little of what they should be put wise to in the only way that he would ever be permitted to by a group of men who control and run about everything in the U.S.A. The People of this great country should be informed of everything and all things that could in any way effect the welfare of their future. But I know there are those in big industry that are hoodwinking the citizens right and left.

I have been obtaining books written independently by ex-reporters of some of the leading newspapers, from the State Library, and I have found out they put into their own books what they never could have given out while they were being gagged by the Capitalists they had been working for. In that way I was put wise to a lot that was going on behind the world's back.

There is some great connection between the Shaver Mystery and the occult. I have a large library of Metaphysical books, among them the Oahspe Bible and Theosophical Works of Leadbeater, Annie Besant and H. P. Blavatsky and I find in the new story, Mandark, the mention of trolls which are also referred to in Leadbeaters "Astral World," I think Max Heindel of the Rosicrucian Fellowship also speaks of the unseen sprites of this earth.

I was unaware that Mr. Shaver received his first awareness of these things in my own State and only a few miles away at that. I got the impression some way that the voices were first heard in Penn. I was indeed surprised to find the scene of discovery so close to home. I can talk to no one except members of my own family about these things for I find the readers of religious works do not read the pulp magazines. I do, because by a peculiar coincidence I was led to the purchase of Amazing Stories just as Mr. Shaver came into the picture. At this time I was a student of Bishop Carl H. Pierce and it seemed to me that here was a force behind it all that was unseen. I am now a student of Dr. Doreal of the White Brotherhood of Denver. Things are becoming a bit clearer but I am still puzzling over the connecting link between these two branches, the caves and the occult, the Elder race and the Mechs. of now.

I keep up a correspondence with the lady in Texas, who wrote the article, "I have been in the caves," and I am sure she is a very sincere and truthful person. She does not, by her explanation, agree with Shaver but there are some things that are not too clear in that explanation. The latch string of my heart is out to any one who is brave enough and wise enough to bring to the people of this world the dangers and also the blessings that have been kept secret for so long.

The 'I AM' books written by Ballard contains a full description of Mt. Shasta's Cave and they correspond perfectly with the stories of Shaver. I suppose you have read these so it is foolish to mention them but I would like to figure out where truth leaves off and fiction begins, or where the trance state leaves off and the actual flesh and blood experience begins.

Please let me know when my next payment is due because this is a magazine that I really want to keep coming. If there is any way I can help to further this great work please let me know right away. If I wrote to you again and asked a very few Questions would you answer me? I do not wish to presume on your time but to me this is very important and I would sure appreciate it if you would kindly take time to answer this. Yours in the search for truth . . . Irene Farrier, Charlotte, Michigan.

Dear Friend:

Main point in your letter is your confusion between what the Occultists teach is true and what Shaver trys to make apparent.

I want to say I have no quarrel with Occult views and they may be true.

But to my eye blaming it all on spirits is a little too much. The caves are made of rock, not wool. It seems to me the Occultists play into the monopolists hands by leaving it all mystic and trans-material, or whatever the phrase may be. They hide the very material value in the caves of which we are all robbed, and they hide the evil selfishness behind that robbery by talking of Trolls and sprites and spirits.

Since I know underworld people, real flesh and blood people, do imitate by projection many of the miraculous visions experienced by Occult believers, I cannot see why all of it is not this same hiding from the light of day a very wonderful treasure of the human race.

A trance is not necessarily caused by a spirit visit, It can as well be caused by a dream-mech, and the dream vision does originate in the records in that mech, or in the mental messages it augments and sends over a ray-beam.

I have seen these things, and see no reason to attribute any of it to spirits, but I could be wrong. There may be spirits at work too. But I am on the material side . . . Shaver

* * *

Dear Mr. Shaver:

I have received and read my first Shaver Mystery Magazine. The theory might be believable were it not for the many discrepancies and contradictions. It seems to follow very closely the course of most mysteries, religious or otherwise.

"Ramon Seti III was bored." Yet, "Around Nydia was all the machinery of a God's pleasures. The very air could be saturated with both nutrient vapor and beneficial vibrants—"

"I am depressed." "Depression", says the Semi-God, "is entirely due to the pressure of 'de' forces upon the mind." Now that is pretty ridiculous for even a man to express. Depression is far more physical than mental. A dose of castor oil or even a hot bath will generally relieve it. And, if 'de' forces from the sun were the cause, why wouldn't everybody be depressed all the time?

The whole theory seems to be constructed chiefly to "lay the blame on George", just as other theories "lay the blame on a Devil." Man is fouly determined to lay the blame of his emotions and misdeeds upon some other person or thing. Why, I have a cousin who grew up in the same locality as myself where, as youngsters, we bragged about whose father was the best at plain and fancy cussin', and yet in later life this same cousin announced out of a clear sky one day that I had taught her to curse.

Mr. Shaver seems to have had this somebody-else-is-responsible complex even before he believed in the caves. "I realized that modern science must have developed a lot of secret things that rich people had got hold of and were keeping from common people." That is pretty corny. It shows Mr. Shaver's natural attitude toward people more progressive than himself. The wicked, wicked rich! They can't even get to Heaven! (The Bible says the same thing.) How is Mr. Shaver going to feel about the rich when he makes a million dollars out of his theory?

Then he tells us about the great health-giving machines which surface people so badly need, and alongside of that he says, the cave people are sometimes blind and have fungus growth etc. But the payoff comes when he states, "Many of the cavern people came of clean and ancient stock that has striven for centuries to make the magic of the caverns the property of surface scientists, of use to everyone," Then, "They had a hearty fear of surface peoples' bungling hands getting hold of their way of their life and ruining their freedom and their secret power completely." Now, do they, or don't they?

I don't see that Mr. Shaver's theory does anything to the God theory, or that the God theory makes impossible the theory of the caves. The caves could very well be inhabited by intelligent people who possess some very wonderful machinery, which is still neither the beginning nor the end. The Elder Race could have once resided in the caves, without being the beginning or the end. Frankly, from Mr. Shaver's description of them, they seem to have been much more ignorant than I had imagined. Their machinery seems to be made up mostly of emotion-stimulating devices, which are certainly of secondary importance since emotion is subordinate to intelligence. But that again coincides with the "mad preachers" who stir their congregations' emotions instead of appealing to their intelligence.

Their records could be as faulty as other records probably are. How real are our moving pictures today? Say, a thousand years from now, would a man see the real way we lived by some of our films?

However I am not bent on refuting Mr. Shaver's theory all the way. And I certainly don't criticise Mr. Shaver for having a theory, nor for broadcasting it. He has had a wonderful experience, whatever the extent of its truth, and, he is doing something about it, which is altogether commendable.

I think though he should change his attitude about what his neighbors might be thinking of him. With his already accomplished success, he should feel a superman. I am sure I would be proud to be his neighbor even if I didn't agree with any part of his theory.

My husband tells me that if I keep writing like this, I will be suspected of being a dero and probably be eliminated from the inner circle of Shaver Mystery fans, but I believe you are inviting honest opinion. I well could write a frenzied delineation of protest against the ungood, unsound policies Mr. Shaver is releasing upon an already harried world but I honestly don't believe Mr. S's theory will do the world any more harm than any of the other theories. Some people always believe. A man has a right to believe. Those who can't believe a spiritual mystery, will no doubt derive a great deal of good out of this. And those of us who believe in ourselves, and so in all people, whether in the earth or on the earth or beyond the earth, will enjoy it for what it is worth to us today. Therefore, it is profitable.

Of course there may be some who become over-zealous and go nuts over it, but it has always been so. Mr. Shaver is at least doing something, and he should be proud rather than self-conscious among his neighbors, who have probably never done an original act in their lives.

So, if the Shaver Mystery goes on the press for further publication, please inform me, as I have another dollar ready for the collection plate . . . Sincerely, Mrs. Loubel Wood, 4017 Melbourne, Houston 10, Texas.

Dear Mrs. Wood:

I like your letter. It shows me I haven't explained myself, and where.

Answering third par.—everybody is depressed all the time, but more so at times because the charge collects like static will collect on a surface. I admit I could know more about "de", but it was their (the Elder Race) prime explanation of evil, and they considered "de" the one big natural enemy of life development. "De" is many kinds of electric—but all have one thing in common, they exert an outward pressure, are disintegrant in effect.

Fourth par. This outbreak of your cousin blaming you for cussing is a sample of what the Elder race called Err—and err was in turn caused by "de" throwing the magnetic flows of thought cells out of alignment, toward ill intent, which they understood as inductive alignment of thought cells with disintegrant energy source, as the sun.

Fifth par. I do sincerely have nothing against the rich for being so. But such samples as Babs Hutton are educational of the pitfalls of the rich. I know that many of our rich are dupes of cavern ray, stim and other things are paid for by them lavishly and they help to keep the secret. For that I blame them.

Sixth par. The cavern people are made of many separate groups, with different backgrounds and customs. They do have fine surgical and health rays, penetray would revolutionize surgery, and it is wasted at present on spy work to keep us ignorant. Their beneficial rays if developed by surface science would make us all much healthier and longer lived. BUT it is confined in the caverns to a privileged few, and the others need it very much, cannot get along in the underworld without it! That is why they look as they do, pale with lumpy skins, rickets as kids, etc. There are those with a hearty fear of surface people because they have an inherited sense of guilt toward us because of the injuries their kind has always done us. There are other groups who want to contact and mingle with us, it would develop both us and them. There are still others, such as powerful rich rulers with harems, who fear the loss of their perogatives although they know that in other ways surface commerce would benefit them. The cavern world has a vaster area than the surface of earth—as it is many tiered.

Seventh par. How do you know that when Jesus said—"My father's house contains many mansions" he wasn't talking of the caverns? The Elder race was far cleverer than I can picture to you. Truth is all our thought contains emotional vibrants—emotional motivations, is always partly emotional. Even when we do our moh, we have a motivation in getting things for wifey, etc. Their science was largely a life-science, and as such they produced all the vibrants of emotion and many others of effect upon life, because they made life rich with the things we only dream of with our emotional thought —they augmented dreams, and dreams are better than mere dull life if you are a good dreamer. To augment a dream, every kind of thought, sensation, emotion must be reproduced. Some cities were ruled with broadcast thought waves, it saved a lot of effort for other things—kept people on their toes. It could as easily be evil rule—but it wasn't

Want to ask you to stick with this till you really grasp all there is to learn about the Elder race and their caverns, as it is biggest thing you will ever encounter, and it is so easy to miss it by scoffing at something that will come clear after you have studied it . . . Richard S. Shaver.